Valerie's Adventure on Slide Mountain

Valerie's Adventure on Slide Mountain

by

REGINA LAMBERT

MOODY PRESS
CHICAGO

ISBN: 0-8024-0320-4

1 2 3 4 5 6 7 Printing/DB/Year 88 87 86 85 84 83

Printed in the United States of America

Contents

1

Confrontation

The bright green Jeep wagon rolled to a smooth stop in front of Valerie Edgecomb's house. She turned to Joanne Peters and Clyde Baker.

"I'll see you guys at the church parking lot in the morning."

They nodded as Joanne's brother Brad got out and opened the door for Valerie.

"I'll be here with Dad's pick-up a little after seven," he said. "I can hardly wait for this snow retreat."

Valerie agreed as she slid out of the vehicle.

"There's been so much pressure on us lately at school and—" she hesitated, glanced toward the house, and continued "—and at home that it will really be good to get away."

"Sounds like you still have a little problem with your dad."

Valerie lowered her voice as they walked toward the house. "I've never seen him so unreasonable before. He won't even discuss my going to Bethel Bible College next year. I went ahead and sent in the preliminary registration forms anyway."

Brad looked at her in surprise. "Over your dad's objections?"

Valerie looked away. "I do have to obey God and not man, and I want to go to BBC. And I *am* eighteen."

Brad jammed his hands in his jeans pockets and scraped the cement with the toe of his shoe.

"Yeah, but—it's not like you, Val." He pulled his hands out of his pockets and hurriedly said, "Well, I've got to go. I'll be here bright and early in the morning. Maybe we'll get some answers from God on this retreat. Am I looking forward to the skiing!"

He turned and jogged down the walk as Valerie called out, "'Night. See you in the morning."

She turned with her hand on the doorknob and waved as Brad started up the wagon. Her three friends waved back as she went into the house.

She stepped into the living room to let her father and stepmother know she was home. A quick glance told her that the two sets of twins must be in bed.

"Hi, I'm home. Looks like you two finally have a little peace and quiet, so I won't bother you either."

"Oh, Val," Carolyn Edgecomb said as she turned down the stereo, "there's a letter for you on the hall table."

Valerie turned toward the hall, but her father's voice stopped her.

"You come straight back in here after you read your letter. I want to talk to you."

Valerie frowned at the harsh tone of her father's voice. She murmured a reply and quickly went to get her letter.

Her heart thumped when she saw the return address— "Bethel Bible College." Quickly she ripped open the large envelope, drew out the letter, and scanned it quickly:

Dear Miss Edgecomb:

We are pleased to inform you that your application for entrance to Bethel Bible College has been tentatively accepted.

Enclosed herewith are other forms and instructions for completing so that we can complete your registration for the fall term.

Valerie smiled happily as she reread the letter and glanced at the packet of forms and instructions. Her happy reverie was broken by her father's voice.

"Valerie, come on in here."

She quickly shoved the papers back into the envelope as she answered, "Coming."

Unconsciously she flipped her long, light brown hair out of her collar and pulled her slim, athletic form even more erect than her normal stance, preparing to face her usually easy-going father.

She sat warily on the edge of a straight-backed chair, purposely ignoring the more comfortable overstuffed one that was her favorite. She looked at the stern set of her father's jaw, a look she had seldom seen. She glanced at Carolyn for some clue to her father's irritation, but Carolyn was nervously picking at imaginary pieces of lint on the couch and refused to look at Valerie.

Robert Edgecomb leaned forward. "I see you got a letter from the Bible college today."

Valerie started to answer, but her father quickly continued, without giving her a chance to reply.

"I told you that I have no intention of allowing you to attend a Bible college, of all things. Not with your scholastic record."

"But Dad," she protested. "Academically, Bethel rates as high or higher than the state colleges."

"Maybe," he interrupted, clipping his words angrily. "In certain subjects."

He drummed his fingers on the arm of the couch. "You are already too deeply involved with religion as it is. If you went to a Bible college you might go off into something crazy."

"Dad, I resent that. My relationship with Jesus is not crazy. It's been everything for me, and it has helped the boys."

"Now just a minute, young lady. I admit, a little religion is good—sort of gives people some moral sense and honesty. The boys have improved since they started going to Sunday school and church, and don't think I'm not grateful that you run with a good clean bunch of kids and didn't get into dope, alcohol, and—and all those other things so many get into. But I'm not going to have you some sort of a religious freak, either. I want you to be a well-rounded person, with a well-rounded education."

"But Dad. Surely you don't think the Peters family is a bunch of freaks, or s—"

"Of course not," he interrupted roughly. "They are fine people, but I think they are exceptions, and for your information, young lady, they are the only reason I have let you get so involved with that church. But I don't know what sort of influence you would come under at some two-bit Bible college."

10

"Dad! It's one of the best—"

"Let me finish."

He stood up and paced the floor, stopped, looked directly at Valerie, then paced again as he spoke.

"Point two, it is stupid, just plain stupid, for you to go to a school with high tuition that is a hundred fifty miles away and pay board and room when there is an excellent state college right here in the city. With the economy the way it is, I'm not sure I can afford the expense."

"But Dad. I've thought of that. I—"

He held up his hand. "I'm not finished, Val."

The room was silent except for the crackling fire in the fireplace. Mr. Edgecomb walked to the fireplace, poked the fire, then sat down next to his wife on the couch. He leaned toward Valerie as Carolyn gazed at her hands.

"Val, honey, we just can't let you move away from home yet. We need you here. The boys need you, and Carolyn has her hands full, the babies are not even eighteen months yet— The boys still count on you. I mean, two sets of twins—that's a handful for Carolyn."

Carolyn Edgecomb looked at her husband miserably. "Robert, please. You make me sound like I can't do my part as a wife and mother."

"I didn't mean that, sweetheart, but, well, those two boys are a handful. Any eleven-year-old boy is, and double that, well, that's trouble. They're used to Valerie. She is a big help."

"Bob, we've been married for over two years now. I'm well, and the boys should be used to me if they're ever going to be. Maybe they won't accept me completely as long as they have Valerie here to depend on."

Valerie sat up, sensing that Carolyn was supporting her, and spoke eagerly.

"That's true, Dad. It is just a habit for them to come to me when I'm around. When I'm gone for a few days, or a week or so, I'm sure they go to Mom for help. What about this summer when I'm going to be a camp counselor? I may not be around at all. Remember, I'll be earning money doing those things. Besides, I have that trust fund. We could get a court order to release some for college, and I can work part time while I go to school."

Her father flushed angrily. "No. You will not touch that trust fund for Bible college. You are not going there, and that's final. You just make your plans for State."

Anger poured through Valerie. She leaped up, glared at her father, and snapped, "Don't you forget that I turned eighteen on my birthday. In this state that means I'm a legal adult and no longer have to be under your control. There are scholarships available; there are loans I could get. Even that trust fund would make collateral for a loan for college. Not only that, I could petition to get it released. Since I am eighteen, you wouldn't have to do it for me. So, you just better think twice about ordering what college I will or won't attend."

Robert Edgecomb clenched his hands as his jaw tightened in anger.

"Young lady, you will not talk to me that way. I'm your father, and what I say goes."

Carolyn jumped up. "Robert! Valerie! Please stop right now. I never heard either one of you talk like that

12

before. Please stop before you both say something that you'll regret."

Robert Edgecomb turned to his wife. "You're right, sweetheart." He looked back at his daughter.

Valerie clenched her hands and bit her lip in frustration.

"Dad, I'm sorry I spouted off like that, and that was wrong—but you're wrong too. I have never seen you so unreasonable before."

Valerie's father glared at her for a second, then set his jaw firmly, dropped back into his chair, snapped open the paper, and said, "This discussion is over."

Quickly he lowered his paper and said, "I let you have your way too long after your mother died. I let you run things around here before Carolyn and I were married."

Valerie's blue eyes sparked with newly aroused anger. She put her hands on her hips and glared at her father.

"You *let* me run things! Dad, how could you say that? Oh yes, it was lots of fun trying to cook when I didn't know how. And it was really a joy to try to keep track of those boys every day after school instead of playing with the other girls. Yes sir, you really let me have things my own way."

Her voice caught as she choked back a sob. "Now that you're married again nothing has changed. You still want a built-in baby-sitter. You don't care about what I want at all."

She choked back another sob and ran down the hall to the sanctuary of her own room, ignoring her father's call.

She slammed her door, shutting off the sound of his

voice, and threw herself on her bed. Tears poured out of her eyes as she sobbed in anger and frustration.

She heard a knock on her door, and Carolyn's voice called to her.

"Valerie, could I come in for a little chat?"

"Yes." She paused, then added, "As long as *he* isn't with you."

Valerie rolled over and sat up as Carolyn slipped in and carefully sat in the armchair in the corner.

"Valerie, I really don't know what to say. I'm sure that your mother would have been able to keep this battle from happening. I wonder if I failed you both by not recognizing that this was becoming such an issue."

Valerie drew a long, shuddering breath. "It isn't your fault, and it certainly doesn't have anything to do with you."

Carolyn nervously twisted her ring around her finger before she spoke again.

"I've never heard you and your father talk to one another, or to anyone else, like that before. We can't let this go on. Can't I do something to help?"

Valerie wiped tears from her eyes and tossed the tissue toward the wastebasket.

"I don't know what you can do. You won't be able to convince either one of us to change our minds."

Carolyn clasped her hands and looked at Valerie.

"Valerie, I don't want you to ever think that you are nothing more than a built-in baby-sitter. We—I love you very much. I appreciate your help, but you are very special to me, and not as my chief assistant."

She paused as though gathering her thoughts.

"That's why I really want to understand what this is all about. Why are you so determined to go to the Bible college when your father is so set against it? It's such an issue, that you, in effect, threatened to leave home."

Valerie took a long breath and closed her eyes. She thought about how to answer her stepmother and how to explain how deeply she wanted to go to BBC, how she just *had* to go there.

"Mom, I'm sorry I spouted off, especially that part about being a baby-sitter. I don't really feel that way. Dad just made me so mad."

"Maybe you said that because deep down you do feel that way. Maybe we've made you feel that way. I have been trying to help take the pressure off you. I'm trying to keep your father and the boys from depending on you so much, but maybe I haven't tried hard enough."

"Oh, Mom, you've done just great, especially since last fall. Please don't blame yourself. I really am sorry for that crack."

"Never mind that for now. Tell me about this college and why it's so important to you. Maybe I can help if I can understand it."

Valerie looked at her stepmother and thought she could see a desire to understand. Thoughts tumbled over in her mind as she tried to decide how to answer. *How can I make a non-Christian really understand why I have to go to a Christian college?*

She bit her lip, then answered, "Could you answer a question for me? Is Dad against Bethel College because it's as far away as it is and expensive, or just because it is a Christian college? If State were a hundred fifty miles away, would he forbid me to go there and make me go to the city college here in town? Or would he let me go to the university instead of State? That would cost me almost as much as BBC."

Carolyn looked away from Valerie's steady gaze before she replied.

"I can't lie to you, Valerie, and besides, you already know the answer. He is completely against the Bible college. The expense really has nothing to do with it."

Valerie nodded. "I knew it. He knows good and well we can get money from that trust fund for college if we have to. That's part of what it's there for."

They sat quietly for a moment before Carolyn spoke again.

"I wonder, Valerie, if just for this first year you could compromise, go to State, just to please your father. The freshman year is pretty basic anywhere. Then, I'm sure, if we work together we could convince him to let you transfer your second year."

Valerie squirmed uncomfortably as she tried to think how to answer."

"Mom, I know that you and Dad don't understand this, but, I have to do what I feel the Lord wants me to do. If I have to disobey Dad to do it, then I will. The only thing I can say now is that I will pray about it, and see how the Lord leads."

Carolyn frowned as she answered. "It's true that I don't understand about being 'led' by God. I believe in God, but I don't believe He's concerned about things like what college you go to. That kind of talk is the very reason your father is against Bible college."

She paused as though uncertain about saying the next words, but finally she continued speaking as she stood up.

"I am a little concerned about one thing. You said that you must obey God even if it means disobeying your father. I'll admit that I don't have the same relationship that you say you have with God, but my understanding is that disobedience to your father would not be obedience to God."

Valerie tensed in anger at Carolyn's slight rebuke.

Carolyn quickly stepped over, kissed Valerie on the cheek, and murmured, "Try to think over what I've said, and see if you can't work something out with your father. Now, I'll go talk to him."

She left quickly, leaving Valerie thinking and half angry.

2
Apologies

Valerie's mind was in a turmoil as she packed her backpack and got her sleeping bag out of the closet for the next morning. She didn't want to go out of her room and take a chance on seeing her father again, so she decided to wait until morning to make certain her ski equipment was ready for the snow retreat.

Over and over she kept praying, "Lord, help me to convince my father that I am right about Bible college."

There was a disturbing thought on the edge of her mind that her prayer was worded wrong. She stopped in the midst of her preparations and thought about it. Then she amended her prayer by adding, "If it be Your will," but that still didn't satisfy the nagging thought that something was wrong.

She finally had everything ready and was showered and ready for bed when she picked up her Bible and started reading. Her mind stayed on her problem more than on what she was reading. She stopped and flipped to Psalms.

She muttered, "I can't seem to concentrate tonight. A nice, soothing psalm is what I need."

She stopped at Psalm 37 and began reading. Suddenly,

she stopped at the fifth verse, and read it again.

"Commit thy way unto the Lord; trust also in him; and he shall bring it to pass."

She read it again. Her heart skipped a little beat and she suddenly felt better.

"Yes, Lord, I will commit this to You, and somehow I know that You will bring Bible college to pass in my life."

Later as she lay in bed, she began to ponder about committing her way to the Lord. Suddenly verses she had memorized about being obedient and submitting to parents began to flow through her mind.

"Lord, I'm sorry that I spoke the way I did to my father. I'll apologize in the morning. Dear Father God, I will trust You to change his mind about Bible college."

Again, there was a little pricking of something slightly wrong with her prayer. Sleep didn't come easily, but finally she dropped into restless slumber.

When her alarm went off, it seemed to Valerie that she hadn't slept at all. Wearily she climbed out of bed and instead of feeling the anticipation of the snow retreat, she dreaded facing her father.

She made sure she was totally ready then, unable to put off going to the kitchen any longer, she quietly went down the hall, hoping that he wasn't up yet.

That hope was dashed the moment she stepped into the kitchen. He was sitting at the table sipping a cup of coffee.

Valerie stopped in the doorway and apologized.

"Dad, I'm sorry about last night. I was out of line, spouting off that way."

He carefully set the cup down and smiled.

"I'm glad you've changed your mind. It's much more sensible for you to go to State."

Anger flared in Valerie again. "I didn't say that at all, Dad. I was only apologizing for getting mad and snapping at you and—and saying things I didn't mean to say. I haven't changed my mind at all."

"Neither have I, young lady. I will not stand for insubordination from you, either, though I am willing to compromise. If you really feel put upon in this household and think you have to get away from home, then perhaps I can send you to the university, but definitely not that Bible college. That's final. The choice is yours, the university or State."

Tears of anger and frustration formed in Valerie's eyes as she tried to think of a retort. *I won't give in to him. I just won't.*

Ralph and Richard, her twin brothers, clattered noisily into the kitchen, interrupting further conversation. Valerie quickly stepped out of their way as they bumped the table.

"Boys," Mr. Edgecomb yelled. "How many times have I told you not to run in the house?"

The boys were quickly subdued by the anger in their father's voice, and they murmured their apologies.

Valeried used the interruption to slip out to the garage to get her ski equipment before she tried to force a little breakfast past the huge lump in her throat.

"Nothing," she murmured to herself, "has been settled. How could he be so unreasonable?"

An unwelcome thought pushed into her mind. *Of*

course, I'm being a little stubborn too. She shook her head. "But I have to follow God's will for my life."

Reluctantly she returned to the kitchen to eat a little, knowing this was going to be a long day. She carefully avoided her father's glances as she ate quickly. Then she hurried to her room to finish getting ready and to watch for the Peterses' pick-up.

As soon as she saw it come down the street, she grabbed her backpack and sleeping bag and hurried through the house.

She paused at the nursery door, where Carolyn was attending to the twin toddlers.

"I'm off for the retreat. Brad's pulling into the driveway now. I'm sorry I upset you so much last night."

Carolyn smiled. "You have a good time, honey."

Valerie hurried on to the kitchen. She glanced at her father.

"I'm really sorry about blowing up, Dad, but I want you to know that I have my mind made up about college."

There was a hardness to his voice as he answered. "My mind is made up too. I don't expect any more discussion on the matter, except for you to decide whether to stay here and attend State or put your application in for the university."

Valerie clamped her lips shut and walked stiffly to open the back door.

Brad grinned and greeted everyone as he took Valerie's backpack.

"Good morning! I didn't expect to see the whole family up so early."

Mr. Edgecomb stiffly greeted Brad. "Morning. No

21

holiday for me today, and these two boys refuse to sleep late."

Valerie pushed Brad out of the doorway. "Let's go."

Brad gave Valerie a puzzled look, but followed her to the pick-up. Mr. Peters was loading her ski equipment into the back and turned to greet her.

"Good morning. You all ready for a great three days?"

Valerie answered, "I certainly am." She thought, *I'd be ready for anything just to get away from this house for a few days.*

She murmured a quick prayer as she climbed into the pick-up. "Please, heavenly Father, please hurry and make my dad change his mind about college."

In the midst of the cheerful talk in the cab of the pick-up, a little thought kept pricking at Valerie. She should also be willing to change her mind if that was the Lord's will at this time. She quickly dismissed such an idea. *I don't see how it could not be the Lord's will for me to go to Bible school.*

The winter darkness slowly gave way to the uncertain light of a cold day as they drove toward the church, towing a trailer loaded with snowmobiles and sleds.

Mr. Peters started giving instructions.

"Brad, I want you and Clyde to start loading equipment in the pick-ups as soon as everyone starts to arrive. Valerie, I want you to help Mrs. Peters check everyone on the list, collect permission slips, and get them seated in the bus as soon as possible. I hope Clyde will be there with Joanne and Mrs. Peters soon after we get there. We have to be ready for the mob."

22

They pulled into the church parking lot just as Clyde came from the other direction.

"Great timing!" Brad exclaimed.

"Not only that," added Mr. Peters, "but look, Roy is here with the bus. We can corral everyone as they come."

Suddenly there appeared to be total chaos as cars arrived and young teens scurried around loaded down with equipment and the allowable baggage.

Valerie and Mrs. Peters quickly directed them toward the bus after they dropped their equipment at one of the trucks. Mr. Peters often stopped by to check their lists and appeared as though from nowhere to help stop a wrestling match that had broken out between two of the younger boys.

At last everyone was loaded on the bus except for Mr. and Mrs. Peters; the speaker, Steve Wagner, and his wife; Roy, the bus driver; Brad and Valerie; Clyde; and Joanne.

Mr. Peters took the clipboard with the names and double-checked it.

"Looks like they're all here. Steve, you indicated you wanted to ride the bus to get acquainted with the young-sters. How about you, Mrs. Wagner? Would you rather ride in a pick-up or on that noisy bus?"

She pulled her coat around her a little tighter against the chilly wind as she replied. "I'll ride the bus. I like to know the young people too. Sometimes I help counsel."

Mr. Peters nodded. "I'm riding the bus to keep order. So, that means, Jo, you can ride with your mother in Clyde's pick-up. Brad and Val, in ours. Remember, boys,

I want you to stay behind the bus. And don't forget, with the bus and two pick-ups towing trailers, we make quite a caravan. Watch for traffic behind us and get over and let them by, especially after we leave the freeway. We're all set. See you at the top of the hill."

They quickly dispersed, and Mr. Peters waved from the bus steps. The bus pulled out of the parking lot. The boys checked their loads one last time and then followed down the street toward the freeway.

Brad drove carefully through the light early morning traffic, watching the bus in front and checking for Clyde's vehicle in the rearview mirror.

Valerie stared out the window and couldn't stop her disturbing thoughts now that she wasn't busy. When they drove up the ramp and onto the freeway, Brad broke the silence.

"You are one quiet gal today. Got something on your mind?"

Valerie thought how to answer him, and then he added, "Hey, I haven't done something to upset you, have I?"

Valerie quickly turned to face him.

"Oh, no, Brad, I'm not mad. It's just the same problem with my father about next year."

Brad glanced in the mirror, quickly at Valerie, and then focused his attention in front again.

"That's tough. I was hoping you had got things settled."

Valerie frowned a little as she answered, "Oh, it would be easy to settle. All I have to do is be a good little girl and say, 'Yes Daddy, I will go to State and not to BBC.' He won't settle for my apology for sounding off like I did. Suddenly he's the heavy-handed father. He wants a complete surrender."

She gave a weary sigh and looked out the window, then shifted in the seat and turned back toward Brad.

"That sounded a little sarcastic, didn't it, Brad? I shouldn't have talked about my dad that way."

Brad glanced at her quickly. "You didn't sound like yourself, that's for sure."

Valerie didn't like the uncomfortable turn of the conversation, but she plunged on, trying to make Brad understand.

"I don't want to fight with my father, Brad, but he just can't see my side at all. There wouldn't be a problem if he'd just give in and let me go to BBC."

"Yeah, that's true, but there wouldn't be a problem if you submitted to him."

"Brad," Valerie exclaimed with genuine shock. "You of all people should know that I have to follow God's will."

"Yeah, I know, but is going to BBC really God's will right now?"

Although a little doubt nagged at the back of Valerie's mind, she stoutly defended herself.

"Of course, it must be God's will. It has to be!"

Silence settled over the two momentarily, then Brad grinned, glanced at Valerie, then back to the highway.

"I have an idea. How about a compromise? See if your dad would let you go to the university. That'll get you away from home. I wouldn't be surprised if he would go for that instead of State. They have a great Christian club on campus. Freshman year is pretty basic, no matter where you go. Then see what happens for the next year."

He stopped, but then hurriedly continued. "Besides,

I'm going to take that football scholarship at the university, and we could still be together."

Valerie turned in the seat and leaned forward so she could look directly at Brad.

"You can't be serious! Not go to Bethel? Brad! I don't believe it. We all thought the Lord was leading you to BBC."

He grinned, and his eyes sparkled as he answered, "I'm serious. Now, do you still want to go to BCC since I won't be there?"

Valerie leaned back and faced forward. There was a touch of anger to her voice as she answered.

"Of course I do. I certainly never planned on going there because of you."

The grin left his face.

"You don't have to sound so huffy about it. What's wrong with you, anyhow? If it's really God's will for you to go to BBC, you shouldn't be so touchy about it."

Valerie turned to the window and blinked back a few stray tears. *Even Brad seems to be against me,* she thought. She didn't trust her voice to speak, though she was aware of Brad glancing her way occasionally. She shifted uncomfortably and tried to forget the thought that was nagging at her.

Could going to State or the university really be God's will for my life for this year? I don't believe it. Why wouldn't God want me to go to Bible college? And who is Brad to be telling me what to do when he obviously is letting his love for football stand in the way of doing God's will and going to BBC?

She shook her head to stop the unpleasant thoughts

and groped for another topic of conversation.

Brad had apparently been trying to find another topic too, for suddenly he spoke.

"Hey, guess who Clyde and I ran into yesterday? I forgot to tell you about it last night."

Valerie turned to him and shook her head.

"Hank Fisher. He's working now at that station on Elm and Broadway. He sure wanted to come on this retreat, but his folks wouldn't let him. They keep a close eye on him since his brother Jerry disappeared like that. Hank's surprised they even let him take that job."

"Don't they have a hint of where Jerry could be?"

Brad shook his head. "Nope. All they know is he was part of that gang of dopers that was responsible for all those burglaries. He's the only one of the bunch that hasn't been caught. He's holed up somewhere. He made a big buy, they say, and just disappeared."

"Poor Hank, having to pay for what his brother did. Doesn't the fact that Hank is a Christian now mean anything to his parents?"

"Not really, Val. They don't understand about that either. In fact they sort of act as though now Hank is going to disappear into some weird group or something.

"He sure wanted to come on this retreat, too. Did you know that he and Jerry and their parents used to come to this lake every summer? He wanted to see what it was like when it was all snowed in."

Valerie replied, "I guess I can understand about his parents. After all, my dad is a little the same way. But Hank really needs the fellowship."

"Yeah. You know what, Val? I feel extra bad about

Jerry, like I didn't try hard enough to reach him for the Lord. I don't know, I just didn't spend enough time with him, didn't go out of my way to get close to him. Then he got in with that other crowd. I sure wish the Lord would give me another chance to really talk to him. I just know I could have done more to keep him from getting so involved with drugs. God knows right where he is, and it may sound goofy, but I prayed a lot last night and again this morning that God would somehow bring us together and give me another chance to talk to Jerry."

"That doesn't sound goofy at all. I think it's terrific for you to be so concerned. But Brad, when you talk like that, how could you decide to accept the scholarship at the university instead of going to BBC?"

"Aw, knock it off, Val. Now you sound like my dad. I like the idea of paying my own way. Dad can't afford the tuition at BBC, even though he keeps saying, 'The Lord will provide,' and, 'Seek ye first the Kingdom of God.' Besides, I figure I can reach guys if I make a name for myself in football."

"But is that what God really wants for you?"

Brad flared up. "What about yourself? You're not really sure either. Maybe God wants you to submit to your dad and go to the university, or State."

Valerie started to retort, then clamped her lips shut, turned, and stared out the side window again.

The silence hung heavily over the two for many miles, each one deep in his own thoughts.

3
Snow Country

As the miles quickly passed, conversation started to flow again, though they carefully avoided any talk of college plans. Their casual talk slowed down again when they reached the snow country and they enjoyed the surrounding snow-covered forest. They drove through the last small community, where smoke poured from the chimneys poking through the snow-covered roofs.

"Wouldn't it be wonderful to be able to live in a place like this?" Valerie said.

"Yeah," Brad answered. "Except it sure looks like there are a lot of snow-shoveling and woodcutting chores around here."

Valerie nodded in agreement when she looked at the shoveled paths and the filled woodsheds as they drove past.

They turned onto a narrow, twisting road that climbed to the summit area where they would park the vehicles and then use the snowmobiles, sleds, and skis to get into the lake area and the lodge that was the site of their retreat.

The sun gave an illusion of warmth as it glared on the snow heaped alongside the road. Occasionally a large fir tree dropped its load of snow, which plopped on the road or thunked on the pick-up. A few wispy clouds cut out the brightness of the sun now and then.

Valerie gave a contented sigh. "It is beautiful out here. I feel so relaxed for the first time in weeks."

"Yeah, it looks great. I can hardly wait to get those skis on and take off cross-country."

Brad shifted gears, and they went into a steeper pitch and into a long, gradual curve, climbing out of the trees. Another curve and suddenly they were at the large plowed area that marked as far as the snowplows had gone on the road.

The bus was already parked, and young people were spilling out. Their bright ski caps and parkas added splotches of color to the white landscape.

Valerie was surprised at the number of cars parked in the area and noted that there was even a motor home.

"I didn't expect to see anyone else here since the lakes and cabin areas are snowed in."

Brad carefully started backing the trailer to a ramp made of snow where others had been unloading snowmobiles. "The people that own cabins at one of the two lakes are using this for winter sports now. There's no down-hill skiing because there are no lifts. But cross-country skiing and snowmobiles are really popular now. A lot of people use their cabins in the winter, too. They have to ski in or ride snowmobiles, like we will. That's the only reason the county plows this road this far."

He concentrated on getting the trailer lined up just right. There was a gentle bump as the trailer went into the snowbank.

Brad grinned with satisfaction. "How's that? Got it right on. Come on, let's unload and then park so Clyde can unload."

There was chaos again as the young people milled around, threw snowballs, and tried to pull their ski equipment off the pick-up before the organized unloading began. They had a lot of energy to run off after being cooped up on the bus for so long.

Once again Mr. and Mrs. Peters used the other adults and the older teenagers to help bring order quickly out of the activity.

Before too long, the group had packs and skis strapped on, the snowmobile sleds were loaded with the baggage, and they were ready for their trek into Lakecrest Lodge.

Mr. Peters gave last minute instructions.

"Stay on the trail; don't go exploring. Clyde and Joanne will lead, but I want you two to remember that most of this group is not as experienced on skis as you are, so don't get in too big of a hurry. Take your time, enjoy the scenery. Remember, this isn't a race. Now, have fun and be careful. Some of us with the snowmobiles will stay behind you in case anyone has any problem.

Valerie watched the skiers go and momentarily regretted that she was now older with near adult status with this group of young teens, and sorry she had agreed to drive one of the snowmobiles pulling a sled full of baggage.

Oh well, she thought as she sighed longingly, *that's the penalty for growing up. Besides, I'll have a chance to do plenty of skiing while we're here.*

31

She looked at Brad and smiled sympathetically, knowing that he too was wishing he had been able to go with the skiers. He grinned back at her and shrugged his muscular shoulders, then turned his attention to checking the baggage and supplies loaded on the sleds. He talked to Roy and Steve, who were also driving, then rejoined Valerie.

"This is what comes of growing old—getting stuck back here with all the old folks."

The roar of two machines coming up the trail caused them to stop talking and look in that direction. Valerie noticed that the drivers' parkas were obviously part of a uniform, and as one of the men turned she saw a sheriff's insignia patch on his arm.

He directed his questions toward Mr. Peters.

"Hi there. That part of your bunch skiing down the trail?"

"Yes, it is."

"Then you must be that church group headed for Lakecrest Lodge."

"That's right."

"Welcome to our winter playground."

"Thank you. We have certainly been looking forward to it."

"Quite a group you have. Just wanted to tell you that if you need any help, grab a snowmobile and come to that motor home parked right there. If we aren't there, leave a note. We check in here routinely looking for messages. We have a radio and can get outside help quick if needed."

Mr. Peters answered. "It's nice to know that help is so

close at hand when you have a group of teens out. I didn't realize you had a resident deputy in the winter."

The older of the two answered.

"We don't normally. People have been complaining that their cabins have been broken into, and we're patroling the area closely right now. Of course, more and more people are using the area in the winter, so even when we stop the break-ins I imagine we'll have someone up here at least on the weekends."

He paused thoughtfully. "Of course, it's not nearly as crowded as it is in the summer. We keep more men up here full time then. It's getting plenty busy in the winter, though."

The other deputy glanced at the sky. "We could have a storm blow in tonight, so if you go out this evening be sure and keep everyone together."

Valerie glanced up and was surprised to see that there were dark, foreboding clouds hanging on the horizon. The wispy clouds had grown fuller and heavier, and there was a slight, chilly breeze blowing.

Mr. Peters responded in surprise. "I didn't think any storm was predicted for this week. The forecast was cloudy, but fair."

The deputy shrugged.

"Predictions don't always mean a whole lot up here in the Slide Mountain area. We seem to have an area here that has its own peculiar weather patterns. When there are clouds coming in like that, there could be snow."

He paused and looked back toward the distant clouds.

"Yep, looks bad. It would be a localized storm, but they can be violent. A person can get lost in one of those as quickly as he can in a statewide storm."

The older deputy nodded in agreement.

"We've had to go after quite a number of people that have gotten caught unexpectedly. Another thing—" He paused, turned, and pointed to an oddly-shaped ridge some distance away.

"See that knob over there? That's Brodie Ridge. It's above an area called the North Fork Canyon, and there's a road that goes right along under it. That's a bad avalanche area there, called Brodie's Slide. Named for a guy that was hauling a sleighload of food into a bunch of miners stranded down on the river about a hundred years ago, in the gold mining days. He got buried by a slide. It's a bad place, particularly when the weather has been like it has this year, perfect for slides and avalanches, especially if the wind starts to blow hard."

Mr. Peters smiled. "Thanks for the warning. I'll keep the young people away from there. There are plenty of other places we can ski and ride. I want you to know that I'm glad you're here. Makes me feel better in case something does happen."

Valerie looked again at the strange ridge, and a shiver passed through her as she thought of the man driving that sleigh and being buried under tons of snow.

She shivered again and jammed her gloved hands into her parka pocket. *Slide Mountain is a good place to stay away from.*

The deputies had returned to their snowmobiles, and with a roar and a wave they turned and headed down another trail.

Mr. Peters turned to Brad and Valerie.

"You two go on now and get on ahead of the group. Get to the lodge and let Mr. Sanderson know we're on our way. Be ready to get that gang organized as they get there. The rest of us will move along slowly and watch for any stragglers."

Brad grinned and eagerly replied. "Right, Dad. Let's go, Val."

They started down the snow-covered Lake Road, which was now a well-marked trail to the lake. Valerie noticed that the dark clouds were now moving across the sky slowly and there were more piling up on the ridges.

They followed the road as it dropped down steadily into the trees again, which grew so densely the sky was almost blotted out. She glanced at the very young trees bent almost double with their tops buried in the snow and wondered how any of them ever survived to grow straight and tall like the huge trees around them.

The road dropped down steadily toward the valley where the lake was nestled, and Valerie wondered if they would even catch up with the skiers, knowing they must be making good time on this slope while she and Brad drove slowly and carefully with their heavily loaded sleds.

The road finally flattened out, and it was darker in the valley with the dense growth of trees and the sun hidden behind the mountains. The cloud cover had thickened, and the air had turned much cooler.

They caught up with the skiers on the flat portion of the road that was twisting and curving around the snow-covered surface that was the frozen lake. They passed slowly, waving at everyone, and stopped when they caught up with Clyde and Joanne.

Clyde leaned his lanky frame on his ski poles and laughed.

"Well, hello. If it isn't the old folks catching up with us."

"Aw, knock it off, Clyde. If Val and I hadn't gotten stuck with this duty you and Jo would have."

"Yeah. I owe you one for that, buddy."

"Dad sent us on down so we can help you get that mob under control at the lodge. Val and I'll go ahead and warn Mr. Sanderson to be ready. At this moment, I'm not so sure I like being the oldest and having Dad depend on us so much."

Clyde grinned. "Oh, quit griping. We'll get plenty of skiing and plenty of freedom once everyone is settled."

"Right as usual. See you."

Valerie and Brad started their machines again as Clyde and Joanne quickly moved with the step, glide motion back on the trail, and ahead of those that had passed while they were stopped.

Valerie and Brad drove carefully and soon caught a glimpse of the large lodge with the steeply-pitched wood shake roof and the huge rock chimneys.

They stopped in front of the building and looked at the pile of snow on the front porch. Only the top half of the massive oak door and boarded-up windows were visible above the snow.

They turned off the snowmobiles and looked up to the second-story deck when a voice called out to them.

"Hi there. Are you part of Mr. Peters's group?"

"Yes, sir." Brad answered. "I'm Brad Peters, and this

is my friend Valerie. Dad sent us ahead to help you get ready for the invasion."

Mr. Sanderson chuckled. "I'm looking forward to it."

He pointed to a path through the snow going around the side of the building.

"The steps to this deck are the main entrance in the winter. Come on up and we'll get organized."

They quickly joined Mr. Sanderson on the deck and conferred about storing the skis and the rooms to assign to the young people as they arrived.

They were ready as the group of skiers swept into the area, followed closely by the other snowmobiles.

Valerie and Brad repeated the instructions over and over.

"Store your skis over there, get your baggage from the sleds, boys go on up to the third floor, grab a sleeping spot, four to a room. Girls take the second floor, four to a room. When you get settled, come down to the main room on the first floor."

The group was just tired enough that they all were a little less exuberant, with less scuffling and teasing than there had been earlier. They quickly obeyed.

Valerie helped Mrs. Peters and Mrs. Wagner see that the younger girls were all settled and then joined Joanne to find a spot to claim as her own. They unrolled their sleeping bags, hung up their parkas, and changed into dry jeans. They hurried down the stairs, checking as they went to make certain everyone else was either gone or ready to go downstairs.

A roaring fire in the huge fireplace in the large main

room cast a warm glow on the log walls and beamed ceiling. It was dark in the room with the windows boarded up, and the only light came from the hissing gas lanterns and the crackling fire.

Mr. Peters called for quiet. "Let's have a quick roll call."

Following that, he outlined the rules, the planned activities, and the meal times.

That evening after dinner, Steve Wagner spoke. The group listened attentively as he talked of obedience to parents, that rebellion was considered the same as witchcraft in God's eyes, and that Jesus had to learn obedience.

Valerie was deeply disturbed by his words. Her thoughts tumbled over one another.

What's bothering me? I am *obedient, more so than most. I haven't given my dad any trouble.*

Her argument with her father about college came immediately to mind.

But, she argued with herself, *that's different. I must put God first.*

Doubt flowed through her again about her choice of college really being God's will for her at that time.

She shook her head slightly to erase the thoughts, reached up and flipped her hair out of her collar, and forced herself to concentrate on what Steve was saying about the different forms of rebellion.

At the conclusion of the teaching and discussion time Valerie found that she couldn't get very enthusiastic about the hot chocolate, snacks, and marshmallows toasted in the fireplace. She slipped away from her friends and went upstairs. There she put on her parka, went out on the deck, and looked over the peaceful, snow-covered forest. She hunched into her parka as a cold breeze nipped at her, and she shoved her hands into her pockets. She was deep in thought until her eye caught the reflection of a dancing light on the glistening snow layered on the ice-covered lake.

Her chill was forgotten as she hurried around the deck to the other side of the lodge. She gasped when she saw flames shooting up into the air some distance away.

She dashed back into the lodge and down the stairs, her eyes searching the main room for Mr. Peters. She saw him in a far corner and quickly worked her way toward him.

Brad grabbed her arm. "Where have you been, Val?"

"There's no time to explain. I have to see your dad."

Brad gave Valerie a puzzled frown, then followed her to the corner where his father was watching everything.

"Mr. Peters, something is on fire out there. You can see it from the deck."

Quickly Mr. Peters and Brad followed Valerie up the stairs to the deck.

4
The Fire

They ran onto the deck, around to the other side, and saw that the flames were shooting skyward and embers were flying in the wind.

"That has to be a cabin!" Mr. Peters exclaimed. "We'd better go see if we can help. Quick now. Get Clyde and Jo, slip into your warmer clothes and boots, and meet me at the snowmobiles. I'll tell Mr. Sanderson and the others."

They scurried to do as Mr. Peters instructed. They quickly found Clyde and Joanne, briefly told them what was happening, and hurried to their rooms to change.

Valerie and Joanne took the time to slip on their ski overpants as well as their felt-lined boots, instead of lightweight ski boots. Valerie grabbed her belt bag out of habit, and Joanne snatched hers too.

The boys and Mr. Peters were already at the machines, pouring in gas and lashing on tarps and other emergency supplies on one sled.

Brad urged his father, "Let's go, Dad. What are you doing, anyway?"

"Just a minute, son. A few minutes right now spent

checking the supplies on the sled might save time or a life later on."

Valerie smiled in spite of herself at Brad's impatience to move as Mr. Peters methodically checked the emergency equipment on the sled and on the snowmobiles. He paused as he took inventory and then went to the other sled, took an extra sleeping bag and extra snowshoes, and strapped them on the sled.

He nodded with satisfaction. "All right, you four, double up on those two machines and let's go."

They drove out to the snow-covered road with a roar and raced through the night toward the fire.

They found a cabin totally engulfed in flames and blazing debris flying all around, sizzling as it landed on the snow-covered roof of a neighboring cabin. The five of them floundered around in the deep snow looking for signs of anyone and double-checking the neighboring cabin to make certain the blazing embers weren't finding any dry piece of wood to ignite.

The fire blazed up with renewed vigor as parts of the large cabin caved in.

Valerie and Joanne met at the snowmobiles and looked around for the others. Mr. Peters walked through the smoke and joined them.

"Did you girls see any sign of anyone?"

"No, there wasn't anyone around at all."

He shook his head with a puzzled frown. "I just don't see how an empty cabin could catch on fire. There's no electricity, so it couldn't be wiring."

Clyde emerged from the trees.

"There wasn't a sign of anyone out that way."

Mr. Peters nodded thoughtfully.

Clyde continued, "Sure a good thing this happened in the middle of the winter. It would have been a nasty fire in the summer. Those other cabins would probably have caught on fire."

Valerie looked around. "Except in the summer there would have been people around to fight it, and there would have been water. I just don't see what would cause a fire like this to start. Wonder why someone else hasn't come around."

Mr. Peters looked around and mumbled, "Now where is Brad? We should report this to the deputies. Apparently the cabins where people are staying are positioned so they couldn't see this fire. I'll go get Brad."

"Hey, Dad," Brad's voice came through the darkness before he stepped into the glow cast by the dying fire. "I found some fresh ski tracks. Someone was here. Let me show you."

They put on snowshoes and followed Brad as he held a flashlight on the fresh tracks.

"They are plenty fresh, and the person on those skis is either a rotten skier or sick or hurt. I found places where he fell down and floundered around getting up. Come on, I'll show you."

They hiked to a place where it was obvious the person had fallen and struggled to get up again. The tracks looked as though the individual was possibly staggering a little as they continued on.

"See. We'd better follow him. That guy needs help."

They hiked back to the scene of the blaze and looked

around the dying fire again, carefully looking for any other tracks.

Mr. Peters said, "There doesn't seem to be any sign of other tracks, and there's nothing to be done for this fire now. There isn't any danger to anything else. Let's go see if we can give that person a lift."

They removed the snowshoes, strapped them on the sled, and started the snowmobiles with a roar. Brad and Valerie took the lead with Clyde and Joanne following close behind and Mr. Peters pulling the sled with the larger machine.

They reached the Lake Road, and the tracks seemed to get lost, intermingling with other tracks. They stopped and looked, then Brad pointed.

"See there, he's fallen again and floundered around. He's probably headed for the cabins around that way. Let's go."

They moved a little more quickly, expecting to catch up with the skier at any moment.

Suddenly Brad stopped again.

"Val," he said, "shine your flashlight up that way."

Valerie's light picked up some fresh ski tracks and also another place where someone had floundered around in the snow and then continued on a side road.

They all stopped and huddled together to discuss the situation.

Mr. Peters stated in a puzzled voice, "That just doesn't make sense at all. That side road goes off away from the lake and cabins where people are. I'm not sure where it goes, but it certainly goes into a wilderness area."

He pulled a map from his pocket, spread it out on the

43

seat of the snowmobile, and, using his flashlight, tried to determine exactly where they were.

"I'm not sure, but that could be the North Fork Canyon Road. It certainly isn't used. That is the only set of tracks."

"Why would anyone go down there?"

"The guy must be sick or confused."

"Don't you imagine he could hear us? Why didn't he stop and wait for help?"

Brad displayed his impatience. "I think we have to go on as quickly as we can. Have you noticed? It's starting to snow. If that guy is sick or hurt, he won't last long out there."

Mr. Peters drew a deep, thoughtful breath before he spoke.

"Brad, I am very much aware that it's snowing, I also can see that there's a problem. But we must let the deputies know what has happened as soon as possible."

"OK, Dad, then let Clyde and me take one of the snowmobiles and follow this guy. You and the girls go back and get the deputies."

Mr. Peters shook his head. "Brad, there's no way I'm going to let one machine go out on that road. What if it broke down? No, that won't do."

The wind began to whip around the falling snow, and Brad said, "Dad, we've got to help that guy, now."

Mr. Peters closed his eyes in thought. "Yes, of course we do. We also need to get the deputies. I don't like this idea much better than yours, Brad, but here's what we'll do."

He looked around at the four young people as though double-checking his idea.

"You four go on two snowmobiles. Take the big one and the sled with the emergency supplies and first aid supplies. I just feel that there is more safety in numbers. I'll admit I don't like this idea, but I can't think of anything else at the moment. You go ahead—I'll go back for the deputies. I'll stop at the lodge and get Roy to go with me. I'm sure you'll have caught up with the skier by then. Load him on the sled and get to the lodge. We'll probably get there about the same time."

He thought for a minute, then said, "I know I checked this sled out before we left, but I want you to know what you have."

"Dad," Brad groaned, "we're wasting time."

"You have to be prepared for any emergency. Now check this over with me."

"First-aid kit, pack with emergency stove and canned fuel packed in a small kettle, cups, packets of dry food, candy, and trail mix. It's not much, but you aren't going on a week-end campout. There's plastic tarps, shovel, small saw and hatchet, fire-starter gelatin, matches, and extra flashlights. It looks like a couple of those plastic emergency blankets, and the sleeping bag."

"Where did the sleeping bag come from?"

Mr. Peters chuckled. "I have learned not to trust the memories of young teens. I brought two extra in case someone forgot. One person did, so I gave him one and put the extra on the sled. It might be a good thing I did, if that person is sick or hurt. You'll need to get him as warm as you can as quickly as you can."

He handed the folded-up map to Brad. "You may need this. Now, one more thing—well, two things: First, I am sure this is that North Fork Canyon Road, so don't go on down into that canyon that goes right into the slide area. The wind is blowing and it's snowing. If you don't catch up with this fellow by then, turn around and come back.

"The next thing is, remember those deputies said that there had been someone breaking into the cabins. This person may not be confused; he might not *want* any help. Don't take any chances. If he doesn't want to be rescued, just let him be and get out of there.

"In other words, anything out of the ordinary, come back and let the deputies handle it."

He looked around the group and especially at Brad. "Do you all understand?"

They all nodded.

Then he added, "The more I think about it, the less I like this idea. Maybe we ought to just let him go and all go back."

"Dad," Brad argued, "if that person is sick, or injured, he could be dead by the time we get up to get the deputies and come clear back here."

Clyde sided with his friend. "You know that's true, Mr. Peters. There is quite a chill factor in that wind."

Mr. Peters looked unhappy as he agreed. "I know. Two, three hours more out here might be too much for that person. Let's pray about this."

The five of them huddled in a little circle as Mr. Peters prayed.

"Father, we come to You for help and guidance at this time. You know that I don't want to let these four young people go on alone, but in our humanness, we can't think of any other way to do this. We are very concerned about that person on skis. He does appear to be in trouble and needing help. Father, You are all-knowing, all-wise, and You know everything that is about to happen. If this rescue attempt is foolhardy and not wise, then please, Father, give us an inner checking in our spirits. We promise at this moment to be obedient, and we will turn back if You tell us to. We ask all of this in the name of Your Son, Jesus Christ."

They stood silently for a moment as the snow pelted on them, swirling a little in the increasing wind. The only sound was the wind sighing through the trees.

Mr. Peters looked around the group and spoke seriously, "Be honest now. Does anyone feel that we should not go ahead with this plan?"

They each murmured in turn, "No sir."

Valerie added, "I feel a little frightened, but I don't feel that we shouldn't go on."

"That's how I feel," Mr. Peters agreed. "Frightened to allow this thing, but I don't get any sense of saying no. So, go with God's blessing, and my prayers. Please be careful; take no unnecessary chances."

The four young people started out with Brad and Valerie taking the lead on the smaller machine and Clyde and Joanne following with the larger one pulling the sled.

Valerie peered through the snow, looking around at the general area and toward the upper slope. It didn't look too steep, yet.

5
The Mystery Skier

The snow pelted down, blowing in the wind, swirling in the headlights of the snowmobiles. Brad and Clyde kept the slowest speed they could to keep going, stopping quite often to check the ski tracks. They found another place where it was obvious the skier had fallen and struggled to get up, but the tracks started again down the snow-covered road, which dropped steeply, and the tracks were straight and true. Valerie noted that the upper bank was very steep now and the lower one dropped off straight down.

"The guy can ski all right. He must be sick or hurt," Brad said, as he climbed back on the lead machine. "Let's go."

They slowly traveled down the road, breaking trail through the deep, fresh snow, watching the ski tracks as carefully as they could with the visibility so poor.

The road narrowed as they started upward again, with the steep mountain on one side and a sheer drop-off on the other. The blowing snow made it more difficult all the time to see what should be the road.

Brad stopped again to check the ski tracks and to check their route.

Worriedly Valerie said, "Maybe we shouldn't go on, Brad. This is getting terrible"

Brad thought a moment before he replied. "Yeah, but we should catch up with him now. He has had to struggle up this grade. As soon as we get around this point it should be better. Right now we're right on the face of the mountain, catching the worst of the storm."

They finished traversing the point and swung back into a canyon that was more protected. Brad stopped the machine and pointed. There in the glow of the headlight was a figure crumpled in a heap on the snow.

Brad and Clyde floundered through the deep snow toward the skier they had been following. As soon as Clyde touched the person, he began struggling and hitting at the boys as he screamed at them.

Valerie just caught the words whipped on the wind, "Leave me alone!"

The struggle was short-lived as the two strong boys held the person. As suddenly as he had started fighting with the boys, he slumped in their arms.

Valerie and Joanne slogged through the drifts to help the boys carry the individual to the sled.

Clyde looked up from examining the young man and said, "He sure needs help. I don't see any injury, but he is sick. Not only that—I—I wonder if he isn't high on something, the way he fought with us."

Brad agreed. "He sure acted strange, but it could just be illness. He isn't dressed warm for this storm, and his clothes are wet. We've got to warm him up.

Brad flashed his light over the boy's face and stared. He looked at Valerie in amazement. *"It's Jerry."*

49

Valerie looked at Brad, understanding the answer to prayer.

"Come on," Clyde said, "let's get him to the sled and into that sleeping bag."

They struggled through the snow back to the sled with their burden. The boys stripped off Jerry's wet outer garments and ski boots, then put him into the sleeping bag. They wrapped a tarp around the bag and settled Jerry on the sled.

Clyde frowned a little as he looked over the narrow area. "I think we're going to have to unhitch the sled and just lift the machines to turn them around."

Brad nodded in agreement.

They worked rapidly in the white world as the wind blew with greater intensity. Snow swirled, making their visibility almost zero.

A loud rumble and crash made them all look up and around as the ground trembled.

Fear clutched Valerie, and she saw her fear reflected on the faces of her friends.

"That was an avalanche," Clyde stated as he looked around.

"Yeah, and it was close, too close," Brad added.

The deputy's earlier warning rang in Valerie's ears. She asked, "If this is the North Fork Canyon Road, could we be on the northeast side?"

"I'm not sure," Brad answered, "but we'd better get out of here."

They finished turning the snowmobiles and started back up the road. They reached the point again, and

Brad stopped. The headlight showed a massive wall of snow blocking the road.

The four friends sat in the midst of the howling storm in stunned silence.

Brad whistled and exclaimed, "Wow."

That one expression seemed to sum up the sight for all of them, because no one added another word.

Finally Valerie asked, "Now what?"

Brad yanked his attention away from the avalanche. "We have to make a quick decision. Now what do we do?"

Clyde flashed his light up the slope, trying to peer through the storm, then grumbled, "Can't see a thing, just was wondering if there's more to come down."

"We'd better not stay too long, but we'd better decide what to do. Any suggestions?"

Joanne spoke up. "Let's go back where it's more sheltered, make camp, build a fire, and wait for Dad and the deputies to get to us."

Clyde said, "That's a possibility, but I wonder. Maybe we can follow this road and finally find a slope that we could ride the machines up, then go across the top, above the slide, and get back down to the road."

Valerie looked around and demurred. "That sounds like a good way to get lost in this storm. We don't know this country. We don't know what we would get into, and we can't see far enough ahead to travel without a road."

"True enough," Brad agreed, "but I don't feel safe sitting here, and Jerry needs help as soon as we can get it for him. Let's look at that map."

They spread the map over the seat of the large snowmobile and huddled over it with a flashlight, holding it tightly as the wind whipped around.

"I think right about there is where the burning cabin was. If so, then this must be the road we are on right now. I hate to say it, but this is the North Fork Canyon Road. But look, it goes on around this way, then there's a fork. It looks like this one goes right on down into the canyon, but this branch goes around to the other side of this mountain and hooks up with Lake Road, way up above where the lodge is. How about it? Shall we try to get back that way?"

The wind whistled and blew the pelting snow into their faces, making them hunch into their parkas.

"I think we had better get off this side of the mountain as soon as we can," Valerie said. "Once we get away from the slide area, we might think about stopping and building a fire."

Brad nodded. "All right, let's turn around again and get moving. I don't like sitting by that mess at all. We could have been under it."

Wearily they started back in the direction from which they had come. Brad was forced to keep a slow pace because the headlight just could not penetrate the heavy blowing snow far enough to allow them to go faster.

They passed the area where they had found Jerry and traveled on, though the way grew more treacherous.

Once again what apparently was the road went back into a ravine, and the wind was not so bad. The snow

now fell heavily, rather than swirling and blowing in the wind.

They had come out of the ravine back toward the face of the mountain again when Brad suddenly stopped the machine. Valerie looked up and forward. The world was nothing but a big mass of snow.

"Wow!" Brad exclaimed. "If we thought the last one was big, look at that."

Valerie closed her eyes in despair. There was no doubt in her mind that this was Brodie's Slide, and the whole area was subject to avalanches. They were definitely trapped.

The four huddled together and held another conference.

Joanne said, "Well, I guess that leaves my suggestion— make camp."

Brad tightened his jaw grimly. "Unless we can find a place to get up the mountainside."

"Boy, it all seemed pretty steep." Clyde said. "But I don't like sitting down here anywhere on this road."

"That deep ravine back there seemed to be more protected. That was the one place where trees came down alongside the road. Let's look it over. First see if there is any way we could drive the snowmobiles up. If not, maybe we could take a chance on making camp right there."

They struggled turning the machines again and all felt weary with the exertion of the long day and long night.

It almost seemed warm by comparison in the deep ravine, sheltered from the wind. They carefully checked around, looking for any area where they could drive off the road and up the mountainside, but the bank was too steep.

Brad mused, "I think we could hike up through those trees, but we'd have to practically carry the sled."

Clyde eyed the area thoughtfully. "We could get the sled up using the rope around the trees to pull it. Yeah, the four of us could do it. Try hiking out on the snowshoes."

Joanne spoke up. "My opinion may not account for much, but Jerry has to have something hot inside of him. It wouldn't hurt any of us either to have some nourishment. I'm for building a fire and a windbreak, getting some hot water, and using some of this dry food we have. Then at daylight see what we can do."

"I think that's a good plan, Jo," Valerie agreed. "I'm sure not too wild about the idea of climbing up that mountain in the dark, in the middle of a snowstorm, dragging a sled. Let's at least wait for daylight."

Wearily Brad nodded his head. "I could accuse you girls of laziness, but maybe you're right. I am worried about Jerry. Maybe some hot soup would revive him."

They all felt clumsy stomping around in the snow, working with gloved hands, but they did work together without much wasted motion. Soon they had the tarps up and a fire going. They piled snow in the small kettle and watched it slowly melt. As they got a small amount of water they added more snow to it.

Joanne shook her head. "I don't think we'll ever get enough melted."

"It is really a slow process, isn't it?" Valerie agreed as she put another cupful in and poked at it with a spoon.

When they finally had enough water, they used canned fuel to try to get it to heat faster and added more snow as the water came to a boil. It took a long time before they had a small kettle full and added dry soup mix and bouillon cubes.

They had hung Jerry's outer garments near the fire to try to get them dry and warm. Clyde kept checking the young man, who still seemed to be in a state of semi-consciousness.

They could hear the wind howling and whipping through the trees, and the tarps snapped and pulled against the ropes holding them fast.

They rested and half dozed until the soup was ready. The boys took a cup of it and roused Jerry, trying to get a spoonful into him. He fought them at first, but began to swallow as they spooned the soup in. Then he began to take the nourishment eagerly. When the cup was empty, the boys laid him down again. The warm soup helped, for he had stopped shivering and now seemed to be in more of a normal dozing state rather than unconscious.

The four friends each had a cup of the nourishing liquid, and Valerie felt grateful for the slight protection from the raging storm, the warm soup, and the fire.

She voiced her gratefulness. "I think we have a lot to thank God for, don't you?"

They quickly agreed with her, and they bowed in prayer. Each offered a short prayer of thankfulness that God had watched over them.

A derisive, slow voice spoke from the sled.

"Hey, I know who you are. You're that bunch of holy

joes that Hank took up with. What're you doin' here?"

"We came up here for a church retreat at the lodge."
Brad answered. "We saw the cabin burning, checked it
out, saw your ski tracks, thought someone needed help,
and followed you. The road got blocked by a snow slide,
and here we are."

"What did you run for?" Clyde asked. "That sure
made it tough on all of us."

There was silence, then Jerry stirred a little and in a
slurred, slow voice answered. "I—I don't know. I don't
remember nothin'." He paused, then continued, "Yeah,
now I remember—a fire. I don't know, maybe I knocked
over the lantern or somethin'. I grabbed that windbreaker.
Yeah, I remember runnin'. Thought someone might come."

Valerie thought maybe he had dropped off to sleep
again when he stopped, but he spoke up again.

"I was having a bad trip, I remember that. I must have
mixed up something wrong. I wanted to hide. I—I think I
remember getting the skis, but I don't remember anything
else, till you strated pourin' that stuff down my throat."

He struggled to a sitting position in the sleeping bag.

"Hey you guys got anything, you know, like—" He
stopped, peered at the group, and answered his own
question.

"Naw, you're all those church freaks, always talkin'
about Jesus. You wouldn't have any stuff. Just my
stupid luck to get rescued by a bunch of holy joes."

He slumped back down, and Joanne angrily snapped
at him.

"You're lucky that it was us. Your doping buddies
wouldn't have had the brains to find you. They're so

56

burned out on that stuff. If they had been as high as you were when we found you, they would have fallen in that snowdrift with you and maybe someone would have found you about next July. Now you've got us all in a mess."

He peeked out of the bag and glowered at her. "You didn't have to do it. I didn't ask you to."

Brad intervened. "Yes, we did have to come after you. We could tell by your tracks that something was wrong. Figured you were sick or hurt, and with it storming like this we knew you were in trouble."

Clyde spoke up as he added some wood to the fire.

"Now that we found you we're glad we came after you. For Hank's sake if not your own. He's really worried about you, and so are your folks."

"My folks, huh," Jerry spat out vehemently. "Let me tell you about my folks."

He squirmed around in the bag. "All Dad worries about is that business of his, and Mom her clubs and causes. Hank is the only one that really cares, then he went and got hooked up with you religious nuts. Left me with nothin'. He wouldn't take stuff any more, or help me get it. There was nothin' left me. I just got a supply and lit out of there, but, man, this last trip was a bummer."

He rolled around in the bag and mumbled a little.

Brad questioned him further.

"Have you been up at the lake ever since you left home?"

"Yeah. Hey, sure you haven't got something on you? I wandered around some. Guys kept getting picked up.

57

Knew I'd have to hole up somewhere. Remembered the great times we had here when I was a kid—" His voice trailed off, then gathered some strength. "Yeah, Hank and I had great times, back when Dad still had time— I bought stuff to last a long time. Then hiked in here. Broke into a cabin."

"When's the last time you ate a real meal?"

"Aw, who knows? I ran out of food, but I still had my stuff. I remember getting hungry sometime, so I started breaking into other cabins around the lake. Took food, matches—just stuff I really needed to get by on. Did take a pair of skis, and boots. Needed them to get around on."

"Well, that clears up the burglaries."

"Hey now, you going to turn me over to the cops? Fine Christians you are. Fine friends of Hank's. Wait till he finds out."

Brad tossed more wood on the fire before he answered. "We have to for your sake and because we are Christians."

Jerry angrily started unzipping the sleeping bag. "Get me my clothes and let me out of here."

Clyde reached out and gripped Jerry's arm. "Hold it, fella. Your clothes are still wet, and there's a storm out there. You'd never make it."

Jerry sagged at the impact of Clyde's words.

"That's better." Clyde released his grip.

Valerie spoke soothingly. "Jerry, Hank is terribly anxious for you. He loves you more than ever now that he's living for Jesus."

Jerry looked into the fire. "Aw, he's not near so much fun anymore."

Brad spoke up. "Know something, Jerry? He's just now found out how to really enjoy life, now that he's found the Lord. Worry about you is his biggest problem right now."

Clyde added, "Jerry, Jesus Christ could change your life so you wouldn't need the dope, or need to run away."

"I don't want to change," Jerry snapped. "Maybe— just maybe—I'd like to be different for Hank, but it serves my parents right if they're upset."

Involuntarily Valerie spoke her thought. "But that's just plain rebellion against your parents. You're ruining your life just to get back at them."

"So OK, that's what it's all about. They don't care, and I'll live my life the way I want to. That's my privilege. So let's quit analyzing me. I guess I'm grateful you came after me—and—and well, I'm sorry if I have us in a mess. I'm sort of thinking a little straighter, and this doesn't look too good. We're going to be all right, aren't we? I mean—well, even the youth authority would be better than—than dying and nothin'."

Valerie barely heard Brad reply, "Jerry, death isn't 'nothin'—" as she went into her own thoughts.

Jerry is hiding behind his parents' failures to excuse his rebellion. I am rebelling against my dad in the matter of schools and hiding behind my love for Jesus to do it. That's what the Lord is trying to tell me—to be obedient, to wait patiently, and He will work things out. It won't hurt me a bit to go to State for a year, or even two, to submit to my dad. If the Lord wants me to go to Bible college, He can work it out. Two years at home would make a big difference, the boys will be older, the babies would be older. Maybe Dad and Mom would become Christians by then. Is this what God has been trying to tell me?

She shivered a little as the wind whipped around their makeshift shelter, even though she had heavy clothes on. She thought again, *Of course, we may be in worse trouble right now than we're admitting.*

She glanced around the little group, silently staring into the fire. Suddenly there was a crashing and a rumbling roar that sounded like it was coming right through their little shelter.

6
Nightmare Climb

The ground shook. Snow and debris roared and crashed so close to them that it spattered their tarps, forcing their shelter to partially collapse.

Valerie's heart leaped into her throat. Jerry yelled as he struggled in the sleeping bag.

"Get me out of here! Get me out of here!"

The four friends quickly pulled the drooping tarps back away from their fire and got out from under them to see what had happened.

"Wow!" Brad exclaimed.

The beam of his flashlight played over a pile of snow with small trees and branches poking out. It covered the area where the snowmobiles were parked. That one exclamation summed up all that anyone could say, for they stood and stared silently at the scene of destruction that had come so close to them.

Valerie glanced apprehensively up the hill, half expecting to see a white wall roaring down upon them.

"That does it," Brad stated. "Dangerous or not, we're getting out of here."

Clyde turned from looking at the mass in front of

them. "Don't you think we need to take time to thank God for His protection first?"

The four gathered in a little circle and held hands as they thanked God for His protection and asked for His guidance for their next move.

Jerry yelled at them. "Hey, get me out of here! What are you doing anyhow?"

Valerie talked to Jerry to calm him down and explain what they were planning to do. He grumbled about the idea of pulling the sled up the slope but admitted he didn't have any better suggestion for getting out from under the slide area.

Then Valerie hurried to help the others gather and repack their supplies and load the sled.

Clyde glanced back toward the pile of snow.

"I wonder if there's anything left of those snowmobiles?"

Brad shook his head. "Hard to tell. They might be mashed, or maybe, by some miracle, they might not have gotten the full force of the avalanche."

"Huh," Joanne remarked. "I'm just glad we weren't on them."

She paused and looked at her brother.

"Brad, are you sure that pulling the sled and climbing up that slope is the only way out of here? What if we hiked down the road and climbed that big slide that's blocking it? Would that be better?"

Brad frowned. "No, because we'd be under the slide area the whole time. This fresh snow on top of the hard-packed stuff and this heavy wind are doing it."

The wind howled and blew snow around them as the trees swayed and bent. The four friends hunched deeper into their jackets for more warmth and looked above them again.

"What—what's to keep the snow from sliding while we're climbing?" Joanne fearfully asked.

"Nothing." Brad answered shortly.

Valerie spoke up.

"Didn't I read that in avalanche country a slope with trees could be regarded as safer because it didn't slide every year? Otherwise the area would be stripped clean every year."

"Yeah, something like that," Brad answered.

"But there are trees in that pile that just came down," Joanne answered.

Brad's jaw tightened.

"We've got no guarantees, sis. Climbing that slope and getting off this side of the mountain as fast as we can is the only thing I can think of."

The boys clambered up to the nearest large tree with the rope, slid back down and tied it to the sled, and made certain that Jerry and the supplies were lashed on tightly.

Jerry protested. "Hey, let me take the skis and climb. I'm good."

Brad shook his head. "Don't think you're in complete control of yourself yet. We'll make it."

Brad climbed the slope, grabbed the rope, and pulled on the sled as the other three pushed and dragged the heavy sled up the steep hillside. They fought the cumbersome snowshoes as they inched upward step by step. They finally reached the large tree, and Brad pulled the rope tight to hold the sled as they all dropped wearily on the snow, breathing hard.

Valerie caught her breath when she heard the familiar rumble and roar off in the distance.

Clyde whistled. "There it goes again. I hope this slope is a lot more stable than the rest of the hillside."

"Me too," Brad agreed. "Let's get on to the top."

He stood up and started untying the rope. Clyde grabbed the sled to hold it. Valerie and Joanne slowly got to their feet and starting helping the boys. They made a harness of one rope for pulling the sled up the more gentle part of the slope.

Clyde slipped the harness on.

"Brad, you break trail. Jo, Val, follow Brad's tracks and stomp the snow the best you can for a track for the sled."

"Don't you want help pulling the sled?" Joanne asked.

Clyde shook his head. "Not here. Maybe if it gets steeper. Best help right now is packing a trail."

The little group started out, Brad leading, picking the best route through the trees. Valerie and Joanne walked in his tracks, trying to pack the snow.

The snowshoes were awkward. It was hard for Valerie to get the rhythm of the straight up-and-down step required and at the same time keep the shoes far enough apart so the inner edges didn't pin each other down, especially going up the mountain. The combined weight of the heavy boots with the liners and the snowshoes pulled on Valerie's legs. She was grateful she kept them in good condition for skiing.

She was so worn out, nevertheless, that she ached all over. It was all she could do just to lift her legs a step at a time, much less think about stomping around to pack a

64

trail. The climb grew steeper and more difficult. She noticed that the trail Brad made now zigzagged, and Valerie at first wearily wondered why, then she realized that it would be easier to pull the sled that way than going straight up.

The climb became a nightmare. Valerie trudged on, stomping when she could force her weary legs to do so. The wind howled and snow swirled around her. She couldn't see, and her legs felt wooden and seemed to be moving on their own. She peered through the swirling snow, and her heart skipped a beat. She couldn't see Brad's flashlight bobbing. She stopped, looked back, and saw only the whirling snow and snow-plastered tree trunks. There was no sign of Joanne. Her mouth felt dry as she flashed her light looking for Brad's tracks. There was nothing ahead of her but unbroken snow. Fearfully she back-tracked, biting her lip, angry at herself.

"How could I have lost the trail?"

A sense of panic welled up in her, and she felt alone and lost.

Stop that, she ordered herself. *His tracks have to be here somewhere.*

She worried about how she had got so far ahead of Joanne. Relief flooded her as her light picked up a set of tracks beside her own, and she knew she'd found Brad's trail. She looked back again and caught a glimpse of two dark shadows looming through the pelting snow. She felt a split second of fright, even though her mind told her it was Joanne and Clyde.

She turned back to them and called out over the wind. "Trouble?"

"No," Clyde shouted back breathlessly. "Just needed another hand on the sled on that last steep section."

Valerie flushed in the darkness, ashamed that she hadn't realized that the last place had been such a hard climb that Clyde would need help with the sled.

"What is wrong with me?" she asked herself. "I lost the trail. I didn't think about them needing help. I've got to straighten up."

Clyde and Joanne stopped next to her, catching their breath.

"Let me help pull," Valerie offered.

Clyde caught his breath before he answered.

"No. Just stay close and use your light to guide us. We lost the trail a couple of times."

Clyde and Joanne gathered up the rope after checking with Jerry to see how he was doing. Valerie flashed the light around, making certain she did have Brad's tracks.

They had just started out when Brad's voice called out.

"Hey, is everyone OK?"

He stepped out of the darkness into the glow of Valerie's light.

Clyde explained. "Took two of us on that bad spot back there. Slowed Jo and me down. Val stopped and waited, then came back looking for us."

Valerie felt ashamed. *They don't know that I stopped because I panicked.*

Brad flashed his light on the group as though to satisfy himself that everyone was there and all right.

"Sorry this is so rough. We don't dare stop until we get on the other side of the ridge. I heard another slide. It was a long way off, but this whole area is unstable. This is too steep to suit me."

"Me too," Clyde said.

They started out again, staying closer together.

Valerie forced herself to concentrate on what she was doing in spite of her weariness.

She thought, *Do the others feel like I do? Have they had moments like I did? It's funny, but even as close as we are none of us would ever talk about it, but we should.*

She noticed that it was growing lighter. She realized that it was daylight, though visibility was still poor in the blowing snow. The world was gray now, with white swirls, instead of black. She looked around and couldn't see the outline of any trees. She hadn't thought the wind could possibly blow any harder, but she was sure that it was the hardest it had blown all night. She felt unprotected and vulnerable and she realized they must be on a bare area. She breathed harder, climbing the sharp rise. It was more difficult than ever to try to stomp a trail.

She peered through the snow. It seemed she could see the top of the ridge, but she wasn't certain. She was having so much trouble just climbing that she knew Clyde and Joanne must be having trouble. She looked up again to see if she could see Brad. She thought she could just make out his figure near an oddly-shaped tree. She turned back toward the sled.

She saw the strain on her friends' faces as they slowly struggled up the hill behind her. Valerie tried to encourage them when she got to them.

"We're almost to the top. I think I saw Brad at the top near a little tree. He's probably tying a rope right now and will be helping. I'll push from the back now."

She floundered in the snow and pushed as Clyde and Joanne pulled. She stepped, pushed, half fell, and repeated the process, thinking they would never reach the top. They moved slowly upward.

Valerie slipped and pushed again, puzzled, for there was such an unstable feeling under her feet. She was sure she detected some movement. She frowned, unable to think as she pushed again.

Suddenly she knew what was happening.

"The snow is starting to slide!" she yelled.

She gave an extra hard push on the sled as Clyde and Joanne tugged and Brad jerked on the rope. The sled jerked away from Valerie, and she felt herself sliding down the hill. The snow pulled her as it slipped down the steep slope. Valerie grabbed for something, anything, to stop that downward pull.

7
Avalanche!

Valerie grabbed only handfuls of snow and knew that nothing could stop her now. Suddenly she felt a strong hand grab her wrist. There was no time to wonder how it was there. She clutched someone's strong wrist and felt a wrenching as the snow pulled at her. Her face was full of snow, and she gagged on a mouthful. She felt another hand grip her arm.

She pulled her other arm free from the snow and tried to grasp something solid with it. The snow pulled harder as it slid down the mountain, and the hands gripped her tighter. She felt as though she were caught in a giant tug of war.

Her mind whirled with half-forgotten instructions she had received in a snow safety class.

If you get caught in an avalanche, get out of your skis, start swimming to stay on top. Swim to the lee side if possible.

She could do none of those things. Her only hope was to helplessly cling to the strong arm holding her and to try to find something solid with the other hand. She waved it around. There was a sharp pain as it scraped across a jagged rock. Her mind registered that this was solid. She clawed at it, seeking a crevice to grab.

Her fingers found a hold. She clung desperately to the rock and the strong wrist as the white force tried to drag her down. There was a wrenching twisting on one leg, shooting pain all through her body.

Suddenly it was all over. She heard the roar and rumble as the snow slid on and gained momentum down the slope, but she was lying on bare, jagged rock.

She felt a gentle touch and Brad's frightened voice: "Val. Are you OK?"

She lay still, afraid to move.

His voice insisted. "Val!"

She drew a deep, quivering breath.

"I—I think I'm all right. I—guess everything is still attached."

Clyde and Joanne joined them and asked their own fearful questions.

Carefully the three of them helped her to turn over. She felt the agonizing pain in her ankle and leg again. She bit her lip and closed her eyes against the stabbing pain.

Joanne quickly asked, "What's wrong?"

"My ankle."

She opened her eyes and glanced at the offending leg. She saw just the shreds of a snowshoe and bindings still clinging to her boot.

"Looks like I lost a snowshoe."

Brad gave a sick grimace. "As long as that's all that's missing and not a leg or arm. You sure tore up that hand."

He wrapped a kerchief around the open wound. "How bad's the ankle?"

"I don't know. It hurts like everything, but—but I hope it's only twisted."

Brad's jaw tightened. "Yeah, me too."

"How—how did you—hold on to me like that? Why didn't we both slide on down?"

He grinned and pointed back behind them.

"That tough, twisted, little tree saved us. After I tied the rope to pull the sled about half of it was lying free. I'd hitched it at the middle—didn't need much more to pull the sled on up. We had all yanked that sled right over the top just as you yelled. I grabbed the free end of the rope and slid to you, grabbed your arm, and hung on. Clyde and Jo grabbed the rope and then each held my legs so I could use my other hand to hang on to you. Teamwork."

Joanne gave a shaky laugh. "I was sure hoping my big brother knew what he was doing when he lashed that rope to the tree in the first place."

Brad got a serious look on his face.

"To tell the truth, I was worried too. I hadn't tied it expecting it to have to hold us against a starting avalanche. Praise God it did hold."

Clyde looked around at the bare rocks and then down the slope where the snow had torn out smaller trees.

"Yes, and praise God we were at the top before it started. It hadn't gained strength yet. If this had happened while we were down there, after it had gained momentum—well—we'd never have made it."

Valerie shivered as a renewed blast of wind hit them.

She wondered if she was cold, or if it was a form of shock. She shivered uncontrollably again.

"Hey," Brad said, "you're freezing. Let's get you off the face of this mountain, out of the full force of the wind."

They carefully helped Valerie to her feet, admonishing her to not put any weight at all on the ankle. Slowly they climbed the very short distance to the tree with Valerie being all but carried by her friends. They moved on to an outcropping of rocks and helped Valerie sit down so she could lean against the rock. The boys moved the sled into the slight protection behind the rock, retrieved the rope, and then all huddled together. They answered Jerry's frantic questions and sat quietly resting their weary bodies.

Joanne stirred and spoke up.

"Know what I was thinking? God planted that tree right here fifty or maybe even a hundred years ago so it'd be right here when we needed it."

Brad looked at his sister in surprise. "Jo, that's one of the most mind-boggling statements I've ever heard from you. The crazy part is, you're right. God has protected us all through this thing, even from our own mistakes."

He looked uncomfortable and looked off into the distance.

"Even from my stupidity. When we got out of the trees I angled over this way. I should have known better. The slope was steep. I could see that. To get out on the bare face of a mountain in avalanche country is a real 'no-no.' Any first-class idiot ought to know better. I should have gone off the other way, where it wasn't so steep when we

72

got out of the trees. My only excuse is I am locked into going this direction because that's the way we have to go. I was stupid."

Clyde clapped his mittened hand on Brad's shoulder.

"Hey, you're doing just great, Brad."

Valerie began to shiver again and Joanne noticed. "Hey, Val's freezing. We've got to do something. Fix a shelter, build a fire."

Brad pushed himself to his feet.

"Yeah, let's make room for Val on the sled and push on. Try to get off this mountain."

Joanne exclaimed, "What do you mean push on? We have to rest."

Brad shook his head stubbornly, but Clyde spoke up before Brad said anything.

"We can't make camp on this bald ridge, so we do have to push on a little way. But as soon as we find a sheltered spot we should make camp. We're all beat. We've got to have some rest and some food."

Brad frowned.

"But we have to get Jerry and Val both off this mountain for some help."

Jerry's angry voice interrupted their conversation.

"You don't have to do nothin' for me. Untie me, give me my skis, and I'll get out of here."

Brad whirled toward the sled.

"Don't be dumb, Jerry. You're in no shape to travel on foot."

"Yeah? I'm just fine. Let me loose and I'll show you."

"Sure," Brad replied, "and let you collapse in a heap like when we found you. You would've been dead pretty

73

quick, lying in the snow like that, no heavy clothes on."

"Yeah? Seems I'm not much better off. You almost got us all killed back there with that slide."

"It's your fault we're in the mess we are in," Brad snapped. "I ought to do what you want. Give you the skis, put Val on the sled, get us out of here, let you go off on your own if you want."

Jerry squirmed around in the bag lashed to the sled.

"Then do it. You'll do me a favor. If you take me back to the lake, the sheriff will take me and turn me over to the youth authority. No thanks."

Brad pulled his attention away from Jerry and looked at his friends. One glance at Valerie and he gave quick orders.

"Come on. Let's shift things on this sled."

They worked quickly, though the wind whipped the snow around, making it almost impossible to see. They moved slowly off the ridge, down the slope. Jerry grumbled and complained about the rough ride and about being crowded. Valerie held on tightly, trying to keep her injured leg from moving. Her hand started bleeding again, and she had to quit using it.

Valerie tried to stop Jerry's complaining.

"Jerry, we'll stop soon and get something to eat."

"I don't need food," he yelled. "I need a fix. You must have some stuff of some sort. You're hiding it. I know you are. Nobody travels without something. Come on, give it to me."

"We don't, Jerry. Really we don't. None of us have any. We don't use any drugs."

He carried on, accusing her of lying, but Valerie was

so tired and hurting so much it seemed like too much effort to try to answer him.

She closed her eyes against the pain, and then opened them again. All she could see was swirling snow, and then she saw the ghostly shapes of a few trees. Hope rose in her that the boys would soon find a sheltered spot so they could stop. She was vaguely aware that Jerry was angrily shouting at her, but she felt so numb she couldn't absorb what he was saying.

The sled stopped. Valerie wanted to get off and see what was happening, but knew it was senseless to try. She impatiently waited.

Finally Joanne stepped up to her side, seemingly appearing from nowhere in the blowing snow.

"How you doing, Val?"

"All right. What's happening?"

"The guys are checking out a spot where they think they can hang the tarps. There's a pile of logs for a windbreak and a thicket of firs near it, next to a big fir tree. Looks good to me, if that thicket isn't so dense that we can't really get set up there."

They waited silently. Even Jerry decided to be quiet. Brad stepped up to the sled.

"It'll be primitive, but we can make it do."

They pulled the sled next to the log pile and started working quickly to put up the tarps, to lay some boughs on the floor of the area, to get some firewood. When the tarps were up Valerie insisted that Joanne help her off the sled to the spot where they were going to build the cooking fire.

Joanne protested. "You stay off that leg."

"I don't have to get on the leg. If you'll help me I can build the fire and start melting snow in a kettle while you help the guys get wood and boughs. I won't be on my leg."

Joanne spread one of the plastic blankets on the snow and helped Valerie sit there. As soon as there was enough wood near Valerie for her to work with, Joanne got the bag of supplies and cook kit and put them near Valerie. She untied all of the ropes on the sled in order to get the bag of supplies.

Valerie filled the pots with snow to start melting it into water. She took the small container of canned fuel and used that to speed up the process. It was a slow task, for it took so much snow to make just a little water, and they must have water. They needed some to drink, and they needed some for their freeze-dried food. Valerie was so thirsty she could hardly stand it. She thought about putting some snow in her mouth, but knew that really wouldn't take care of her thirst, and she was already so chilled she couldn't stand the thought of the cold snow.

She was glad to see the pot over the canned heat had melted all of that snow and was steaming. She added a little more snow, and it dissolved almost immediately. It seemed like a major victory to her that there was water there.

Joanne brought in another pile of small wood for the fire and left again. She could hear the boys off in a distance. She didn't hear or notice Jerry moving around. The first that she was aware that he had left the sled was when he suddenly grabbed her and flung her aside. Pain shot through her leg, and she cried out. He grabbed the

76

pack and shook it, dumping the food and emergency supplies all around. He hit the kettle and spilled the water. A package of dried food fell into the fire. Valerie grabbed Jerry.

"Stop that, Jerry!"

He yanked his arm free and grabbed her. "Where is it? Where did you hide it?"

He pushed her to the ground and grabbed her throat, yelling, "You tell me now. Where is it?"

Valerie twisted and turned, pulling at his hands, trying to break his grip on her throat. She looked at his glazed, angry eyes and knew that he was capable of doing any terrible thing right then. She cried out, "Help!" His hands squeezed and she struggled and gasped as her breath was choked off.

8
Snow Camp

"Please," she gasped.

Another voice screamed. "Brad, Clyde, help!" There was a haze across Valerie's eyes, but she saw Joanne leap on Jerry and pull on his hands. For an instant the pressure on her throat was even stronger, and Valerie was sure her windpipe was going to be crushed. Then the pressure eased, and she started gasping for air. At that moment she heard an angry roar. Unexpectedly Jerry was jerked off and Joanne rolled to one side. She saw Brad yank Jerry to a standing position, ball up his other hand into a fist and hit Jerry on the point of the chin. Jerry collapsed in a heap.

Clyde entered the shelter and whistled.

"What a shambles! What happened?"

Brad and Joanne were both busy attending to Valerie.

"Val, are you all right?"

"Val, if that guy hurt you, I'll—I'll kill him."

Valerie rubbed her throat, then reached out to Brad.

"Don't even talk that way, Brad. I'll be all right. He really didn't know what he was doing. You should have seen his eyes. He really didn't know. He was out of his head."

Clyde joined the others and asked again. "What happened?"

Brad carefully helped Valerie to a sitting position as he answered Clyde.

"Jerry went nuts again. Remember how he was when we first found him, how strong he was? He went crazy. Probably looking for drugs."

Valerie answered, "He kept asking 'Where is it?' but where did he get the strength? I couldn't handle him."

"Drugs make people do some weird things," Clyde said. "Sometimes they do have extra strength."

Valerie looked around. The cooking fire was out, the pots were both knocked over, and the water gone into what had been the fire. The packet of supplies was scattered all over, the plastic blanket was ripped, and a package of food was smoldering in the edge of the fire. One of the tarps had been pulled down, and they all sagged. Jerry was crumpled in a heap in the midst of the mess.

Valerie looked at the smoldering fire and the empty kettles. Tears of frustration filled her eyes.

Brad saw the tears and gruffly said, "He did hurt you."

She shook her head, not wanting Brad to do anything in his anger.

"No. Really. It's just the spilled water. It takes so long to melt snow. We are all so tired and need it so badly."

Brad gently wiped a tear from her cheek.

"Everything's going to be OK."

Then he leaped up, motioning for Clyde to help him. They carried the unconscious Jerry to the sled, zipped

79

him into the sleeping bag, and tied him down.

Brad shook his head.

"What a rescue mission this has turned out to be. A dopehead that doesn't want to be rescued, and now *we* need to be rescued. We're not sure where we are—can't seem to get a decent shelter built—"

His voice trailed off, and the four worked silently and quickly to repair the damage.

Valerie's hand was bleeding again, and her ankle throbbed with pain. She didn't dare put any weight on it, but she worked with her friends the best she could to repair the damage to the shelter and fire and to get snow melting again.

Joanne got the first-aid kit while they waited for snow to melt down, and the boys went out for more wood. She cleaned and wrapped Valerie's hand and then covered the fresh bandage with the handkerchief to keep the gauze clean.

The boys strung some of the rope near the fire in the front of the shelter and hung their parkas and outerpants up to dry. Valerie shivered a little without her parka, though she was right in front of the small cooking fire. She kept adding snow to the little bit of water in the kettle.

Brad wrapped one of the plastic blankets around her shoulders.

"Sorry we had to take the parkas, but we had to dry them so they will be good and warm again."

Clyde said, "This isn't exactly ritzy accommodations, but not bad, considering."

Valerie looked around their tiny shelter and silently

agreed. The tarps on three sides and over the top broke the wind and protected them from the falling snow. The sled was right in front of the pile of logs, with the tarp between so that it wasn't even blowing with the wind. The tarps on the sides were popping and billowing, but the boys had tied them well, for they were holding. The front of the shelter was open, but that was where the big fire was, radiating some warmth. There were green boughs on the floor of the small space to protect them a little from the snow. The small cooking fire inside the shelter gave quite a bit of heat for its size.

They huddled close to the cooking fire and rested for a few minutes.

"We'd better look that leg over real good, Val." Brad said. "See what we are really up against."

They carefully removed Valerie's boot and gently probed the ankle and lower leg.

Clyde seemed satisfied as he sat back. "Of course it's impossible to tell until it can get X-rayed, but my guess, for what it's worth, is that you twisted a tendon. They hurt like everything. We'll keep you off of it as much as possible."

They wrapped it to give it some support, and Valerie put her boot back on.

The fatigued group sat quietly, adding snow until they had the two pots full of water. Their stomachs growled as they anxiously watched, waiting for the water to start bubbling.

Jerry began moaning and groaning. Clyde and Brad looked at one another.

Clyde said, "I almost forgot about him. We should

have checked him a long time ago."

Brad grumbled, "I deliberately forgot about him."

Clyde leaned over Jerry. "Are you all right?"

Jerry groaned. "Man, my chin sure hurts. Did I bump it or something?"

Clyde glanced at Brad and said, "Or something."

Jerry strained against the ropes, trying to sit up.

"What do you mean, 'Or something?' Untie me. I can't move."

Clyde checked the ropes to make sure Jerry was not tied too tightly. Satisfied that he could move around, Clyde moved back to the fire before explaining to Jerry.

"You sort of went out of your head a little while ago—probably a flashback, or something. You—you attacked Valerie, so it's safest for all of us if we tie you down."

Valerie was so weary that she just couldn't sit any longer. She lay on the boughs near the fire and listened to the snapping and crackling of the fires, the howling wind popping the tarps, the trees sighing and creaking. She heard her friends talking. She dozed a little, but was too hungry and too uncomfortable to really sleep.

Clyde quietly said, "If it would just quit snowing we could see a ridge or something to establish just where we are. Then maybe we could find the shortest route out of here on the map."

Joanne added, "If it quit snowing they'd probably have a plane up looking for us. All we'd have to do is signal them and wait for rescue."

"*If* it would quit snowing," Brad grumbled. "How long can we wait? What we ought to do is eat, leave Jerry here, take the sled for Valerie and hike on out of here. I think we can find our way, even in the storm."

Clyde and Joanne both started speaking, but Jerry's voice interrupted them.

"That's what I've been telling you. Give me my skis and some supplies, take your sled, leave me alone. You're not any good for me. You got no stuff. You'll only turn me over to the cops when we get to the lake."

"OK, wise guy," Brad yelled at him. "Take your skis and get out of here. See how far you get."

Valerie pushed herself to a sitting position.

"Stop it, both of you! Brad, you know better than to talk like that. What's got into you? Jerry, you wouldn't last through tonight in that storm, and you know it. We're all in this together, and we have to work together."

"I'm sorry," Brad apologized. He put a few sticks in the fire. "He sure makes me mad, but that's no excuse, is it?"

"You've worked so hard, Brad. I understand."

Jerry snorted. "Where's all this so-called Christian love Hank used to tell me about? You, Brad, have picked on me and griped at me, and you all plan to turn me in. I know it."

Clyde carefully said, "If we hadn't had Christian love and compassion, we'd never have kept on looking for you in the first place. You'd never have survived the night."

"Maybe that would have been best after all. I can't stand going without a fix, and I sure don't want to go to jail. Maybe dying's better than jail."

Clyde spoke patiently.

"That wouldn't be better. You aren't ready to meet God."

"Yeah? I don't think God exists. So there."

Brad's voice showed his irritation. "You'd better believe He exists."

Valerie broke into the building tension.

"Look, the water is bubbling. Hand me the soup mix and that chocolate mix. We're going to eat soon."

Conversation ceased as they stirred the contents of the pots and laid out the utensils from the pack.

When it was ready Brad and Clyde took a cup of soup to Jerry. They untied him and pulled him to a sitting position and offered him the soup.

"Take that junk away. I want some stuff, some good stuff, not that junk."

Brad tightened his jaw angrily and balled his hands into fists. Valerie's heart started pumping faster, fearful that Brad would do something he'd be sorry for. She started to speak, but Clyde spoke up first.

His voice was quiet, but firm. "Jerry, you listen to me. We didn't come out here just to have you die on us for lack of nourishment. Now you start eating this, or I'll pour it down your throat."

Valerie was astonished at Clyde making such a threat, but obviously the quietness and firmness of his voice had an effect, for Jerry silently took the cup of soup and started eating it.

They silently ate, too tired and hungry to talk, enjoying the hot soup and chocolate. When they finished, they cleaned up the utensils, refilled the pots with snow, and set them over the fire. The boys took the garments off the line in front of the fire and decided they were dry. Valerie gratefully put her parka on, put her ski pants under her, and wrapped the plastic blanket around her the best she could.

She watched the boys tie Jerry down to the sled again as Joanne settled on the boughs next to Valerie.

"Hey, you can't do that," Jerry protested. "It's uncomfortable. I won't do nothin', honest I won't."

Brad ignored him, but Clyde answered.

"Sorry, Jerry. You might not mean to, but we can't trust you. We've got to have some rest. This is the only way we can do it, until we're sure you're really all right."

Brad grumbled as he lay down.

"We shouldn't be wasting what is left of the daylight."

"You're right," Clyde answered, "but we've got to rest. If we could have rested a little last night, then we could go on today. Of course, it's snowing so hard that we could wind up traveling in circles anyway."

"Maybe," Brad said, "but I still think we should be traveling."

Joanne sleepily murmured, "Not without me kicking and screaming, we don't. I've had it. You'd have to drag me out by my hair to get me to move right now."

Brad chuckled. "That'd be fun."

The silence that settled over the group contrasted strongly with the raging storm outside the shelter.

Valerie's hand and ankle hurt, and she stirred around uncomfortably. Every time she moved a sharper pain shot up her leg, so she forced herself to lie quietly. The cold seeped up from underneath her in spite of the boughs and plastic blanket. She dozed, heard someone moving around adding wood to the fire, and she dozed again. Just before she dropped into a deeper sleep she thought that the storm sounded like it was growing stronger instead of weaker. The wind shrieked with a higher pitch, the trees creaked louder, and the tarps snapped vigorously.

Her fitful sleep was violently interrupted by a loud crack. Instantly, something crashed on the edge of their shelter, pulling the side tarp down. The top tarp dropped over them and into the small center fire. They struggled against the tarps that engulfed them, fighting to free themselves. They scrambled around, crawled out from under the tarp, and stamped out the flames on the one that had dropped into the fire. They cut away the one that had caught from the big fire and stamped it out as well.

Jerry screamed for help.

Valerie felt again as though she were in some sort of a nightmare in a totally white and cold world with the muffled, unreal cries.

They freed Jerry from the tarp that had fallen on him, then covered him to keep the sleeping bag dry.

They looked in awe at the huge limb that had broken from the tree and crashed on the edge of their shelter.

They worked as quickly as possible in the swirling snow, their feet sinking in whenever they got off the boughs, and gathered all of their supplies into a pile.

Then they huddled together under one of the tarps, near the blazing fire.

"Now what?" Joanne asked. "Do we build this shelter up again?"

Brad looked at his sister. "Now that we have rested a little, and since we have lost this shelter anyway, I say let's get off this mountain."

Clyde frowned. "Are you sure you know the right way? We could just be heading right into some canyon."

"Let's look at that map again," Brad said.

They dug out the map and spread it on the ground near the fire. They all studied it and discussed where they might be.

Brad sat back thoughtfully. "I admit that I don't know where we are, for sure. But I am sure we want to go that direction. Maybe we can at least find a better place for shelter. I vote we move."

"Whatever you think best," Valerie said. She really wasn't listening to the conversation around her after that as she concentrated on the map in front of her, thinking that there might be some clue to really help them know exactly where they were. She didn't see anything, but she tried to imprint details on her mind in case they needed to know later on. She prayed silently for help and thanked God once again for His protection.

"OK, gang, let's load the sled, make room for Val, and get moving."

"Brad, you use the skis and let me use your snow-shoes."

"No, Val, you're going to stay off that ankle as much

87

as possible. Give it a chance to heal a little."

Valerie argued some more, but when they started out, she was loaded on the sled with Jerry and the supplies.

The group trudged through the snow in what they hoped was the right direction. Each time they had to go around some thicket of trees or other obstacle Valerie worried about their going in the correct direction again. Then she wondered how they were so sure they had even started out in the right way. Night came on, and very soon Valerie couldn't see anything. She wondered how her three friends could possibly see, but remembered their hike the night before, and the flashlights.

Even Jerry had quieted down, and Valerie was left alone with her thoughts. She felt so helpless, like an extra burden, and she didn't like the feeling at all.

The sled stopped. Valerie looked around but saw nothing but blackness and swirling snow. Brad stepped to the sled, breathing heavily.

"How you doing, Val?"

"I'm fine, but how are the three of you doing? Please let me walk now. It would lighten the load for you."

Jerry spoke up. "Better yet, give me my skis and let me go."

"No to both of you," Brad answered. "We're trying to decide what to do. It's tough traveling in the dark. We have just come to a small stream. Jo suggested that we find a spot to camp near it so we won't have to melt snow for water."

Valerie quickly agreed. "That's a good idea."

She cringed at his next words.

"Glad you like it. Joanne can wait here on the sled with you, and Clyde and I will go look for a spot to hole up."

Her heart pounded a little faster at the thought of being separated. *What if they get lost, or can't find us again? What if they get hurt?*

She started to voice her fears, but Brad spoke quickly, as though reading her mind:

"It'll be OK. We won't go too far. We'll stay close to the stream. If we can't find a more sheltered spot, we'll do the best we can right here."

Before she could even think of a way to argue against the idea, Joanne joined her on the sled. They had to move Jerry around to make more room, and he grumbled about being uncomfortable having to sit up. The boys covered them with one of the tarps and the girls huddled together for their wait.

They sat silently, for a long time, listening to the wind and snow. They began to feel chilled just sitting.

"Val," Joanne asked, "what do we do if—if they don't come back soon? I mean, shouldn't we build a fire or something? We can't sit like this all night. I'm getting cold already."

Valerie tried to sound more confident than she felt right then. "They'll be back soon."

They waited, silently dealing with their individual worried thoughts.

Valerie knew that Joanne was right. They couldn't sit like that all night. They had to have a fire.

She thought, *I know Jo and I could get some sort of a*

windbreak and a fire built. If my ankle would hold up. But should we do it? What if the fellows have found a good spot? We'd have to tear it down and move—all that extra work.

She grew impatient and more worried, for they had been gone so long. Valerie started clicking on her pocket flashlight more often to check her watch. The cold seemed to be seeping right through her jacket and ski pants, and she was very hungry again.

Jerry squirmed around and impatiently grumbled.

"Hey, come on girls, show some sense. Those guys are lost or something. Untie me and I'll help build a fire and shelter. That'd help the guys—if they get back."

Joanne agreed with Jerry. "He's right, Val. Let's build a fire, get some water heating."

Valerie was tempted. Jerry did sound like he was rational and not going to cause any more trouble. She knew he must be very uncomfortable tied as he was. She thought again of that terrible look in his eyes when he had grabbed her around the throat, and she felt fear rise up again as she asked herself, *But what if he should go so crazy again, when the boys aren't here? I wish I knew more about what drugs do. I just don't know what to do right now.*

Valerie shifted her uncomfortable position and scrunched deeper into her jacket.

Joanne urged, "Val, I'm cold and hungry. we can't sit here all night. It would help the guys for us to have something hot for them when they get back."

Valerie thought of the logic of doing as Joanne asked,

They could do it, but they'd have to untie the ropes to get the supplies off the sled. Could they really trust Jerry? He seemed all right, but there was doubt nagging at Valerie.

Silently she prayed, *Oh, heavenly Father, please give me wisdom. I don't know what to do.*

9
The Cabin

The wind whipped the snow and tugged at the tarp. The girls clutched at the tarp, but the wind pulled, and cold air blew on them.

Joanne's voice shook with the cold. "Val, we have to do something. We can't keep on like this. I'm freezing."

Jerry said, "Yeah. I'm not doing as bad in this bag as you gals, but we need a fire."

Joanne slid off the sled. "I'm going to untie Jerry and this load. I'm tired of waiting, and we have to have a fire."

Valerie frowned. She didn't like the idea, but she was too tired, cold, and hungry to argue any longer. Her feet sunk into the snow as she slid off the sled, and there was a slight pain in her ankle. The full blast of the icy, wind-driven snow hit her, and she shivered. She moved to Joanne's side. They started working on the first knot. Valerie caught a flash of light out of the corner of her eye.

"Wait, Jo, I saw something."

She looked in that direction but didn't see anything. She watched intently as Jo fussed, still working on the knot.

"There, look, Jo, I did see a light. Look, it's the guys."

"Quick, undo those ropes!" Jerry urged the girls. "Hurry."

Valerie excitedly said, "No, the boys are coming. Maybe they've found a place to move to."

"Hey," Brad called out. "We found a cabin!"

The girls excitedly questioned.

"A cabin? Where?"

"What's a cabin doing up here?"

"Is it near Lake Road?"

"Whoa." Brad laughed. "Hold it. It's just a dinky old makeshift cabin, not someone's vacation home. It will offer the barest shelter. But it's dry. It has a stove, table, and bunks, no mattresses. They look homemade, built right on the wall. Must just be used in the summer. The two windows are boarded up, but the door was locked shut with an outside bolt so anyone could open it, instead of a padlock."

He paused to catch his breath, and Clyde continued.

"The stream is close by, so we'll have water. We took time to build a good fire in the stove so it'd have a chance to get that chunk of iron good and hot and start warming the cabin. It's primitive, but we can hole up there until the storm is over."

They joyfully moved again, following the stream down the slope. They crossed a tiny flow of water joining the other stream. It seemed much farther to Valerie than she had thought from the way the boys talked. As they continued she wondered what had made them keep going this far. Finally the sled stopped. Brad and Clyde helped her off the sled and half carried her into the dusty and

93

dirty cabin. Mice scurried out of sight as they entered. It was warm in comparison to the temperature outside. The boys helped Valerie to sit on the wooden plank floor and ordered her to stay put until they had the sled unloaded.

Joanne came in with an armload of the tarps, and the boys came quickly, carrying Jerry, bag and all. Clyde looked at the fire while Brad hurried back out to the sled and got the rest of the supplies.

Valerie nervously watched Jerry as he squirmed out of the sleeping bag, but he quietly started helping stack some wood by the stove as the boys brought it to the door of the cabin. Valerie got to her feet and stood for a moment as the sharp pain stopped, then helped Joanne get out their supplies and start heating the water the boys had brought from the stream.

The bunks had webbing, like lawn chairs, instead of springs. They put the tarps and plastic blankets on them and decided that would have to do. The boys brought in some green boughs to put on the floor for the sleeping bag.

The mixture of dry soup and bouillon cubes was finally ready, and the very tired group sat quietly sipping the hot food and soaking up the warmth from the roaring stove.

Brad set his empty cup down and spoke apologetically.

"Jerry, I owe you an apology. I've let my temper get the best of me several times. I haven't shown any Christian love to you at all. I've yelled at you; I slugged you when I didn't have to. I haven't been an example of what Jesus wants me to be at all."

He hesitated and squirmed around a little before he continued.

"So, right now, I'm telling you, and I'm telling Jesus I'm sorry. I know that Jesus is forgiving me, and I wish you would too."

Jerry looked at him then looked away. "I guess I have to forgive you—you've saved my neck, so I owe you one."

"Jerry," Brad said, "I was just praying the other night for a chance to talk to you. If you'd give your heart and life to Christ, He'd forgive you and help you lick the drug problem, and change your whole life. The only difference between you and me is that I've asked Jesus to forgive me for my sins, and you haven't."

"Aw, shut up. I don't believe in your God, I don't believe in Jesus, and I don't want to be preached at."

"But, Jerry, think what it would mean in your life, and think of Hank. It'd be a new life for you."

"Yeah? I don't want a new life. Just leave me alone, will you?"

He sat on the sleeping bag, paused before he crawled into it, and spoke a little more calmly.

"I'm grateful you pulled me out of that snowbank and have taken care of me. I just don't want any of this Jesus talk. My brother and I had a good thing going until he got hooked on Jesus. That Jesus took the only person I cared about from me."

He started crawling into the sleeping bag.

"But Jerry," Brad said, "if you'd give your heart to Jesus, you and Hank would be closer than ever."

Jerry ignored that last statement, crawled into the bag,

and turned his back to the group.

They sat silently, each thinking about Jerry and his attitude.

Suddenly he turned over, sat up, and faced them.

"One thing you can do for me. If we find Lake Road ourselves, or if a rescue party comes, just let me have my skis, this bag, that pack, and let me slip off on my own."

Brad firmly said, "We can't let you do that."

"Yeah," Jerry snapped, "that's what I thought. Fine Christian you are. Listen, all rescue means for me is the youth authority and jail. If you really cared about me you wouldn't want that to happen."

Brad answered, "That might be the best thing for you. Get you off the drugs. Get you started to a better life."

Jerry didn't answer. He plopped back into the bag and flipped toward the wall.

Brad glanced at Jerry, closed his mouth, and stood up to put more wood in the stove.

Clyde stood up and yawned. "Let's get to bed. Won't be the most comfortable, but we're all so beat I bet we sleep anyway."

They helped Valerie get to her feet and they all crawled onto the bunks, the girls on the lower ones and the boys above.

Joanne mumbled, "If we're still here tomorrow night, and if my parka is dry, I'm going to sleep in it. I'm not warm enough right now."

"Better than that snow camp, though," Valerie answered groggily.

They were so exhausted that they all slept deeply in spite of their discomfort.

Valerie jerked awake and lay for a second wondering what had awakened her. Then she realized she was hearing a loud whirring noise she couldn't immediately identify. She sat up and realized how chilly the cabin was. Her next thought was that they had all slept so hard they had let the fire go out. She still puzzled over the roar she was hearing. She frowned, then suddenly she was awake enough to know what she was hearing.

She leaped off the bunk yelling, "A helicopter! Quick, there's a helicopter."

A sharp pain shot up her leg as she put her weight on her injured ankle. She almost fell, but gained her balance and limped across the floor to the door. She jerked it open and tried to see the helicopter. The noise was fast fading away, and the trees surrounding the cabin blocked her view of the sky.

Discouragement swept over her, and her shoulders drooped as she vainly searched and listened for any sign of the helicopter's returning. Brad and Clyde joined her at the door.

Brad hit the door frame with his fist. "If only I hadn't let the fire go out. Maybe he would have seen our smoke."

She scanned the cloudy but snowless sky, praying that the pilot would turn this way again. They couldn't hear it at all now.

Clyde said, "No use, he's gone. We'd better get inside— get the fire going again."

Valerie glanced at Jerry sitting up in his bag, leaning against the wall with a satisfied smirk on his face. He didn't look the least bit sleepy. She had a thought. Without thinking, she made an accusation.

"Jerry, you were awake, weren't you? Did you hear that helicopter? Why didn't you wake us up, run out and wave, or something?"

He smiled and lay down without answering.

Brad took a few quick steps and reached down and pulled Jerry to a sitting position.

"Is that true? Were you awake?"

Jerry shook his head, then he stopped, his eyes gleamed, and he smugly answered. "Sure. I heard them coming. I knew the fire was out, so figured they'd be gone before you could do anything, you were all so zonked."

Brad's jaw tightened, but he released Jerry and strode across the cabin and out the door. Clyde finished building a fire.

Joanne sleepily sat on the edge of the bunk and mumbled, "What's going on?"

Valerie sat down on the bunk and explained what had happened.

Jerry sat up and defended himself. "I told you that rescue only meant jail for me. I didn't want that thing landing anywhere near here until I could get away."

Brad stomped back into the cabin with an armload of wood and dropped it next to the stove.

He jammed his hands in his pockets as he faced his friends.

"No sense in blaming Jerry. It was my fault for sleeping so hard I let the fire go out."

"Brad, no," Valerie said. "It's not your fault. We were all too tired. They'll be back. We'll be fine right here until they do."

Joanne exclaimed, "Hey, either my watch is crazy or

it's afternoon! How could we sleep half the day away?"

Brad slumped against the wall. "Nothing wrong with your watch. That's just what we did. I can't believe we did it, though. How could I do such a thing?"

"It was easy," Clyde answered. "We were exhausted, and our bodies finally said that was enough."

No one spoke again while they worked at getting a skimpy breakfast ready from their dwindling food supplies. When they finished eating, Joanne spoke up.

"Is there any chance the 'copter might come back this way?"

"Doubtful," Clyde answered. "They're probably going to concentrate on the North Fork Canyon road, then go back a different way to cover a larger search area."

"But if the storm has stopped, won't they keep looking?"

Clyde's voice was tinged with disappointment when he answered her question.

"Sure, when it does finally stop storming. It hasn't stopped. That was just a break. The clouds are dark again, and the wind is building up. We're in for it again for a little while anyway. The chopper has probably already gone back."

Brad got up, looked out the door again, and faced his friends.

"I'm going to get those skis and go get help for all of us right now. While it's not snowing, I ought to find the way out of here. I'm going to check that map right now."

He rummaged in the pocket of his parka for the map as Clyde stood up.

"You're not going out there alone, Brad."

Brad clapped his friend on the shoulder. "It's the only

way. I could make a lot better time. I can get help and bring them back. Besides, we can't leave the girls alone with Jerry, unless we tie him up, and I hate to do that."

Jerry leaped up. "Why can't you trust me? Sure I went nuts yesterday, but I'm OK now. I got a better idea, though. Let me leave on the skis. Or, better yet, you all go, leave me the bag and some food. It wouldn't be bad pulling just Valerie on the sled."

Brad shook his head. "Be reasonable, Jerry. You couldn't make it alone, and what would you do here alone?"

"I've been getting by alone for a long time. I could make it. I won't go to youth authority, I'm telling you right now. I won't go to jail!"

Jerry dropped on the bag, Clyde pushed his cowlick back while Brad silently traced an invisible pattern on the floor of the cabin with his toe. Valerie watched everyone tensely, sensing tempers ready to explode. She tried to calm the situation by making a practical suggestion.

"It's late already. The storm could start up again any time. No one is going to find us here tonight, but we have shelter, heat, water, and some food. Let's rest tonight, see what the weather looks like tomorrow. Does that sound reasonable?"

"Yeah, I guess," Jerry said, "for now. But I could make it on my own, from here. I know—" He stopped suddenly.

Valerie thought, *Does he know the way out of here? What has given him the clue? The stream?*

Brad paced as he answered. "You're right, of course, but I don't like just sitting here. So much could happen."

"Oh, Brad," Joanne grumbled, "you never like just sitting. We're all worn out. It's silly to take off this late in the day."

Clyde went to the door, opened it, and looked out. "Too late anyway," he said. "It's snowing again."

Brad joined his friend at the door. "We'd better get out there and drag some more wood in, and get more water, while it's light."

He dropped the map on the table without looking at it, and put on his parka. He looked back at Jerry and then at the girls.

"Will you two be OK with him?"

Jerry exploded, "I'm sick of this! Let me have my skis back, and I'll get out of your way."

"Brad, Jerry, stop it, you two. Brad, we'll be just fine. Jerry, you can help us right here."

Joanne grinned as she got into the discussion.

"Besides, Val and I could handle Jerry."

Jerry frowned, but Brad laughed.

"Yeah, you probably could at that. If you were ready for trouble. Let's go, Clyde."

The two boys left, and Jerry sat on the sleeping bag sulking. Valerie tried to talk him out of his bad mood while she and Joanne spread out their remaining food on the table to see what they had left.

Joanne shook her head. "We'll have to be even more careful with what's left. We don't know how long it's going to last."

Valerie frowned and spoke more to herself than to Joanne. "I thought there was more. I can't be sure, but it looks like something is missing. I can't tell what."

Jerry spoke up. "Probably lost some back there when our shelter collapsed. It was pretty confusing."

Valerie answered doubtfully. "Maybe."

Her mind whirled as she thought about the missing food. She tried to remember exactly what had been there last night. They were so tired.

Jerry walked to the table and looked at the supplies.

"Looks about right to me," he muttered. He casually picked up the map and took it to the sleeping bag and spread it out.

"How would you know what should be here, Jerry?" Joanne said. "You haven't done any of the cooking."

He shrugged but didn't answer.

Valerie thought again. *He is acting strange. Would he steal some? And now studying the map. Would he really be so silly as to try to sneak away?*

She decided there would be no point in making any accusations. She got busy trying to clean things up to get ready for the night meal, such as it would be. She glanced at Jerry, studying the map and nodding as his finger traced a section.

Joanne said, "Hey, Val, let's change the bandage on that hand while we have time."

Valerie watched Jerry as Joanne worked on the hand, puzzled and disturbed because he had such a satisfied gleam in his eye as he looked at the map.

He knows where we are, she thought.

She said, "Jerry, can you figure out where we are, from the map?"

He folded it up. "No. I thought I might, but I couldn't figure anything out."

He lay down and turned his back toward them.

He's lying, Valerie thought. *He saw something on the map that meant something to him. What?*

The boys returned with the sled full of wood, and Jerry went to help them stack a lot of it next to the stove while they stacked the rest near the door. Valerie took that opportunity to pick up the map that Jerry had laid on the floor halfway under his bed. She spread it out and started searching in the dim light in the cabin. She didn't know what she was looking for, but she scanned the area.

The boys stomped the snow off their feet and entered the cabin. Jerry walked by, saw Valerie, and stopped.

"That won't do any good. It didn't help me a bit, and I know this country better than you do."

Casually he started folding it up. "We'd better clear the table so we can get a meal cooked, hadn't we?"

Anger stirred in Valerie, and she started to protest, but stopped, knowing that any little thing could spark another battle between Jerry and Brad.

She refused to relinquish the map, though, when they finished folding it, and slipped it into the pack bag.

The two boys stripped off their outer garments and hung them to dry before they dropped wearily to the floor. Valerie realized for the first time how much strength had been drained from the two powerful, athletic boys.

They had exerted so much energy the last few days, in so much cold and with so little food.

She had thought everything was all right when they found the cabin. But how long could they hold out? The food supply was so low. How much longer was the storm going to last? What if they all got too weak to go out and get wood? Without heat, without food, how long could they last?

She closed her eyes and leaned back against the rough wall of the cabin.

Lord, help us. We could still be in real trouble.

10
Trapped in Flames

Silence settled over the group in the cabin as the wind shrieked around the eaves. The old wood shingles rattled in the heavy gusts. Cold air seeped into the cabin in spite of the roaring fire in the stove.

Brad stirred restlessly and went to the door, opened it, and then quickly pushed it shut again when snow blew in.

"Wow, that's some blizzard out there. Worst it's been yet. We're never going to get out of here."

He dropped on the floor as Clyde answered him.

"Maybe it'll be a lot better tomorrow. You know how a storm sometimes rages the worst just before it stops. We can make decisions tomorrow. Don't have to think about it tonight. Man, I'm too tired to even think."

They sat quietly, listening to the raging storm, and finally Valerie broke the silence.

"Speaking of decisions, I've made an important one. Jerry helped me make it."

Jerry sat up. "Me? What are you talking about?"

Valerie laughed. "You rebelled against your parents, but I did too. Oh, I kidded myself and used serving God as an excuse, but now I see what God has been trying to tell me. Everything I've been reading in the Bible lately, now that I think about it, has been showing me I should submit to my dad and trust God to work things out. Then, Steve talked about the different forms of rebellion there are."

"But, Val, what are you talking about?" Joanne asked. "You've never rebelled against your parents."

"I think I know what she's talking about," Brad said. "Go on, Val."

"I refused to even consider going to State because I figured that since my dad isn't a Christian he couldn't possibly know what's best. I was so sure that God wanted me going to Bible college that I was determined. That determination wasn't following God—it was rebelling against my dad, wanting my own way."

She paused, and no one interrupted her this time.

"I was getting ahead of God. I know that eventually I will go to BBC. Carolyn was right. I can go to State for a year, live at home, help out there, and let God work on my dad. When the time is right, I will go, but not in stubbornness and rebellion, but with God's leading, and no bad feelings between me and my family."

Joanne smiled. "That's great, for me. Sure, we'll go in different directions, me being in high school and you in college, but we can still get together. Not like it would be if you were gone to BBC."

Jerry grumbled. "That sounds dumb. If there is a God, He wouldn't care where you went to school."

Brad stood up.

"God is real, and God does care. Our parents sometimes make mistakes, but God said we are to obey and to submit. Their mistakes are honest mistakes, because they

106

really want what they think is best for us. If we trust God, and obey our parents, He will help them correct their mistakes. He'll work in their lives—and work in ours. Sometimes we make mistakes, too."

Clyde stretched out his long legs. "Quite a sermon. But you're right on the mark."

Brad jammed his hands in his pockets and looked at the floor. His friends knew he had more to say, and they waited.

Valerie flipped her hair out of her collar. A quick thought passed through her mind. *I think I'll get it cut— maybe get a whole new hair style before I start at State next fall.*

Brad spoke again.

"I've made a decision too, and Jerry helped *me*. I saw how messed up he is. God spoke to me again about the work that needs to be done to help young guys before they get hooked. He's been calling me to do that for a long time, and I've ignored it, sort of."

Jerry interrupted. "You all make me sick, talking about God like He's real, and guiding you. What's wrong with taking stuff? I like it."

Brad turned to Jerry. "You're lying about liking it, and you know it. You're lonely, you're scared of jail, scared of dying, you're trapped. Jerry, God is your only hope, if you'd just listen."

"The only thing I want," Jerry said, "is to get away as soon as it stops storming. I won't go to jail."

Brad shook his head, "Where could you go? You wouldn't even get off this mountain. Even if you did, then what?"

Jerry stood up. "Listen, wise guy. I know exactly how to get off this mountain. I'm strong enough now, too. Maybe as strong as you, now. I've had it easy, you've fed me, I could make it."

Joanne gasped. "Jerry, do you really know what direction to go?"

Jerry smirked, crawled into the sleeping bag, and turned his back to the group.

Brad grimly tightened his jaw, sat down, and slumped against the wall, silently admitting defeat in finding out any more from Jerry.

Valerie smiled at him sympathetically, knowing Brad was disappointed at Jerry's response. But God wasn't finished with him yet. She thought about the map and wondered again what Jerry had found that had pinpointed their position. She thought about getting out the map and looking at it again.

Tomorrow, she said to herself. *Tomorrow. I'm just too tired tonight.*

"Hey, Brad," Clyde said, "You never finished telling us your decision."

"Oh, yeah." Brad shifted, trying to get more comfortable.

"Way deep inside I knew that God wanted me to go to BBC to prepare for His call to minister to young guys. But they don't have a football team, and it was going to be tough financially. Then I got this terrific scholarship offer from the university. I convinced myself that I could get the basics there, and build a name for myself in football, that this would make young kids listen to me better, you know, be a sports hero and they'd look up to me."

He stopped and looked at the rest of them.

"That's what God does want—for some guys. I could name a bunch of them. But I know now that's not what He wants for me. Who knows, maybe football would be so important it'd turn me away from God. I know now that my dad is right, too. I'm going to BBC. Not sure how we'll work out the finances, but Dad and I will work on that together.

He glanced at Valerie and grinned.

"Once I made up my mind, I hoped you were going to stick to your decision to go to BBC. But I'd rather have you following God's will."

She smiled. "Maybe it's best if we don't go to school together for a year or so."

"Yeah. God doesn't make mistakes. But I sure hate to break this gang up."

They sat quietly, thinking about their plans.

Clyde spoke up, trying to console Brad about losing out on football.

"Bethel has a great basketball team. You could probably make that. Or what about track?"

"Sure," Brad agreed. "Besides, I'll be a lot happier participating in those things and being in God's will than I ever would be playing football. And not only that. The scholarship would be great, but what if I got an injury, even in practice? That might finish the scholarship. Sure, God knows best, and I have to trust Him all the way."

"That goes for all of us," Valerie added. "All we have

to do is have enough sense to trust Him."

They all sat quietly then, deep in their own thoughts. Valerie closed her eyes and listened to the howling wind. The fire sounded comforting as it snapped and popped, though she felt a little chilly leaning against the wall.

They decided to get on the bunks and try to sleep, hoping the storm would blow itself out and they might be able to decide to travel again, or maybe even the helicopter would come.

Valerie and Joanne both decided to sleep with their jackets on. The boys had to leave theirs hanging because they were still damp from being out in the storm gathering wood.

Valerie lay down with her boots on. "My ankle is so much better, but I'm still afraid to take my boot off."

"Go ahead," Brad said. "Even if the foot and ankle swell, and we decide to try to hike out, we could pull you on the sled."

She shook her head. "No, I just don't want to chance it. It might be uncomfortable, but I have a feeling it's the best thing to do."

The others quickly dropped off to sleep, but Valerie squirmed uncomfortably. She didn't know how long she lay awake, tired but unable to still her thoughts and get her body in a comfortable enough position to sleep. She realized the fire had died down a lot. She got up and limped to the stove and added wood, using her pocket flashlight to see in the dark cabin. She returned to bed and finally dropped off to sleep.

Something woke her later. She lay listening, heard

someone moving around, and thought, *Someone is adding wood to the fire.*

She dropped off to sleep again. A draft of cold air made her wake again. Her mind registered that the door had opened, but again she went back to sleep with the thought *Someone checking the storm.*

Her mind just barely registered that the wind was still howling. She wondered when the storm would finally blow itself out. She slept again, restlessly.

Suddenly she jerked awake, coughing. She opened her eyes and saw a flickering light reflected on the wall. She was puzzled. What could be causing the light? She coughed again. She turned over, toward the inside of the cabin. Her eyes popped open, and her heart leaped in her throat. Flames danced on the opposite wall, shooting up, growing in strength. She realized she was coughing because the cabin was full of smoke.

"Fire!" she screamed. "Fire!"

She leaped out of bed and fell as she put too much weight too suddenly on her injured ankle. She scrambled to her feet.

She yelled again. "Fire! Get up!" She grabbed the small kettle full of water and threw it on the flames, but it was too late. The fire snapped and roared, and Valerie limped to her bunk, grabbed the tarp to beat at the flames. She shook Joanne. "Quick, the cabin's burning!"

Joanne sat up groggily, then sprang into action when she saw the flames.

She joined Valerie to try to beat the flames down.

"It's no use!" Valerie yelled. She looked back and saw

the boys still in the bunks.

She yelled again. "Brad! Clyde! The cabin's on fire."

She and Joanne hurried to shake them awake. Suddenly Valerie realized they weren't asleep, but unconscious from the smoke. Being in the top bunks, they had been breathing it for some time.

They jerked and pulled to drag the boys off the bunks. They each hit the floor with a thump and mumbled a little.

Valerie was thankful the distance to the door was short as they dragged the boys to the door. She tried to open it, while Joanne went to waken Jerry. The door wouldn't budge. She pushed on it again.

Joanne yelled, "Val, he's gone! Jerry's gone!"

Valerie shoved on the door with all her might. It bulged, but wouldn't open. Joanne helped her, and this time it creaked, but it still held fast.

"Jo, it's no use. There's a drift against the door!"

The flames shot higher, and the roof began to blaze as the girls pushed against the door, trying to force it open.

Valerie cried out, "God, help us. We're trapped!"

11
A Voice to Follow

Valerie and Joanne coughed as they threw themselves at the door again. It held fast.

"The window!" Valerie shouted.

She grabbed a large piece of wood and beat on the boards nailed across the window. Joanne joined her with a piece of wood, and they both beat on the boards. They coughed, and Valerie's eyes stung as the smoke swirled around them. The boards splintered, and the fire behind them flared up anew.

Joanne boosted Valerie through the window, yelling, "Hurry, open the door."

Valerie dropped into the deep snow and struggled to get out of it. She tried to get some solid footing. The more desperately she tried to hurry, the deeper she sank into the snow. Tears of frustration and fear filled her eyes as she floundered and struggled to get around the end of the cabin to the door. The roof blazed, and flames shot into the air. The short trip seemed to take an eternity.

She found she could actually move faster crawling. She reached the door and scooped away snow. Hot embers dropped around her. She fell back as the door suddenly gave way and Joanne burst through.

Valerie rushed inside, grabbed a tarp and rolled one of the boys on it, and started dragging him out. Joanne helped her, and they quickly were rushing in to get the other one. They rolled him on the other tarp and dragged him out.

Valerie spotted the snowshoes leaning against the cabin, and she flung them away from the cabin so they wouldn't burn. Then she and Joanne dragged the boys farther from the blazing cabin.

It was useless to try to go back and get anything else from the cabin. It was totally engulfed in flames.

She looked at Joanne. "Are you positive Jerry was gone?"

"Yes," Jo replied with a shaky voice. "I checked again after I boosted you out of the window. He and the sleeping bag were gone. Let's move the sled."

They struggled through the snow to the sled and pulled it away from the side of the cabin, feeling the scorching heat as they did so.

Pulling the sled, they floundered through the snow, fighting it step by step, until they got to where they had left the boys.

Much to their relief, both were stirring and regaining consciousness in the fresh air.

They brushed the snow off the sled and helped the two shaky boys sit on it. They wrapped the tarps around them. She noticed for the first time that Joanne didn't have any boots on.

"Jo, your feet! Oh, Jo, sit on the sled, get them out of the snow—your boots."

Joanne glanced down with a puzzled look. "I—I forgot

I didn't have any boots on. I didn't think to slip them on, I was in such a hurry. Oh, Val, what are we going to do? We don't have anything. Everything's burned up."

Valerie shook her head with a worried frown.

"I don't know."

Brad's voice was weak as he asked, "Wha—what happened?"

Valerie hesitated, then answered, "The cabin caught on fire somehow."

Clyde sat up. "How?"

Brad looked around. "Where's Jerry? Didn't he get out?"

Joanne snapped. "He got out all right. He's gone. So is the sleeping bag, and the skis. When we tried to get out, the door was blocked with snow. He must have left a long time ago."

Valerie looked back toward the cabin. The fire was dying down, though a few limbs on trees near the cabin were burning. She shivered in the chill air, and felt thankful that the wind wasn't blowing, nor was it snowing.

Suddenly she realized they would need a fire. She floundered through the snow to where she had tossed the snowshoes and strapped on a pair. Then she hurriedly gathered some wood, piled it up near the sled, and hiked back to get a flaming piece and put it on her woodpile. Soon it was blazing and giving the needed warmth.

She hiked around, gathered more wood, and then sat near her friends to rest.

Joanne asked, "What do we do now?"

"Pray," Clyde said. "That's all we have left. No way we can move anywhere, we have nothing left, we can't even build a decent shelter. We need a miracle now."

Brad agreed. "If they don't find us today, we've had it."

Valerie stood up. "You all stop talking that way. We can't give up. There is something we can do. I don't know what, but something."

She piled more wood on the fire and limped around gathering more, thinking the whole time. It was growing lighter, and she felt that surely with daylight they would think of something.

"It has stopped snowing. Maybe the helicopter will come again. Surely he'll see our fire."

She gathered green boughs, the best she could, wanting to have them to make more smoke.

She sat to rest again and watched the dark sky turn to a dull lead gray of heavy clouds hanging over them.

So much for the helicopter idea, she thought. *If that cloud cover doesn't break, they won't be up in the air today.*

Except for the pain in her ankle she felt numb all over. Vaguely she wondered if this was what death felt like. She glanced at her friends and saw them all lethargically staring into the fire. She thought about Jerry and felt angry at him. Thinking of Jerry, she thought again of the map.

What did he see that made him so sure he could get away by himself? I know that was him I heard. As soon as it quit snowing he started gathering things to go. What does he know that we don't?

She heard her friends' discouraged talk and knew they had given up. She shook her head. *We just can't,* she thought. *We have to do something.*

She closed her eyes, thinking about the map—there was something there, but what? She pictured it in her mind, and all at once it was vivid. The stream. She remembered that when they had gone into the lodge by the lake, they crossed a stream. There was a small bridge. It wasn't obvious, all covered with snow, but she remembered it. She thought again about the map. Were there other streams? Probably, but this must be the same one.

Suddenly she was sure it was.

She stood up, strapped the snowshoes on again, and stated, "We won't give up. There is something we can do, and I'm going to do it."

She gathered more wood, trying to keep from limping. She placed the green boughs in front of the sled. All the time one or the other of her friends was admonishing her to "sit down, rest, maybe the clouds will break and the helicopter will come."

Finally, she gathered one more pair of snowshoes and stood back from the group, ready to announce her plan.

"I am sure that stream leads to Lake Road. I'm going to follow it and get some help. None of us would survive another night out here like this. You can't hike; you have no boots. The clouds are too thick and too low for the helicopter to fly. I have to hike out. That's what made Jerry know where we were and how to get out of here—the stream. Well, I can follow it too."

"Valerie," Brad demanded, "sit down. I won't let you go."

"How are you going to stop me?"

Valerie stepped back as Brad stood up and lunged

117

forward. She hiked away as he floundered in the snow. She stopped and watched.

"Please, Brad. You're only getting your socks wet. Listen to me. I have my heavy jacket, boots, and snow-shoes. I have that little flashlight and a few matches. I'll stay right with the stream. If someone finds you first, they can come after me. With the stream, I know right where to send help."

She threw the other pair of snowshoes toward them. "Here, you can't go far with no boots, but they may help you if you have to get more wood."

She started hiking away from the group, into the white wilderness, alone. She was tempted to turn back. Her ankle throbbed already. She didn't feel so sure that she was doing the right thing, but she bit her lip and grimly kept walking, slowly but steadily. She trudged on, staying near the stream. The wind started blowing slightly again, and the clouds seemed darker and heavier.

Valerie prayed. "Please, Lord, give me strength to get to Lake Road. Please hold back the next storm to help us out of this mess."

Doubts filled her mind as she hiked on, her ankle hurting with each step.

Unexpectedly she came to a sheer drop. The stream rolled and rumbled as it cascaded into a waterfall. She felt fear and uncertainty leaving the stream and hiking through the forest, searching for a more gentle slope. She looked to see if she was making deep enough tracks in the crusty snow that she could follow them back if she got lost.

She caught her breath. She crossed ski tracks.

"Jerry!" She looked around, then followed the tracks a little way. There was no sign of another set, where he might have turned around. Fearfully she looked around again. "Maybe these are coming up, coming back, not going away. What would happen if I ran into him? Would he really try to hurt me?"

She stopped as she answered her own question.

"Of course. We're the only ones that know it was Jerry breaking into cabins. Mr. Peters only knew that 'someone' was around; the deputies only knew that 'someone' was breaking in. Only we know it was Jerry. But—would he really try to hurt us?"

She remembered the panic of trying to break through the door while the cabin blazed. She didn't know what Jerry had determined to do, but she knew she couldn't forget about him again and had to keep a careful lookout.

She saw that the tracks started down, and she decided to follow them, trusting that Jerry was more interested in getting away than looking to see if they had followed him.

She trudged on, carefully, straining to hear any unusual sound, anxious to be able to locate the stream again. She had to stop often, but the cold wind chilled her and forced her to move on.

The slope leveled off, and she got into some brush and lost the ski tracks. She moved in the general direction of the stream, desperately anxious to find it again. She got through and over the brush patch, into the fir trees again.

She glanced at her watch and was horrified to see it was now afternoon. She tried to move faster, but was not

119

even sure she was moving in the right direction. She was so tired she just wanted to drop on the snow, close her eyes, and sleep.

She heard a noise. Her heart pounded harder. Her mouth felt like it had cotton in it. She had one thought. *Jerry.*

Like a frightened, hunted animal, she scanned the area looking for a place to hide. She slipped into a thick group of fir trees and hid behind one that was bent over in the snow. She sat down and tried to quiet her breathing as she waited.

Three deer moved past her thicket. She couldn't believe her eyes.

"I thought they all always left the high country in the winter." She relaxed as she watched them, realizing they had made the slight noise.

She sat back and relaxed. It felt so good to just sit there. The trees even protected her from the wind a little. She closed her eyes. *I'll just wait until someone comes along.*

Suddenly she sat up. *What am I doing?*

She forced herself up and moved on, downward and always toward where she hoped the stream was.

At last she found it again. The stream had grown in size since she had left it. She knew it was being fed by springs and maybe other smaller creeks or streams. She felt more confidence now that she was following the one that fed into the lake.

"Unless," she said worriedly, "unless we are clear on the other side and it's feeding into the North Fork. No! We couldn't have got that far off. We must be on the side of the mountain where the streams feed into the lake, not the river."

She closed her eyes, trying once more to visualize the map and to remember the different drainage areas.

She took a drink from the stream and followed it again. She hurt all over now—she was so weak and tired. Her body moved as though it belonged to a robot, step by weary step. She felt detached from her body and the world, except she was aware of constant pain.

She reached another steep place, not as bad as the waterfall area, but looking very difficult to climb down. She sat and pondered her problem. It was growing dark now. She didn't have much daylight left. She was afraid that if she left the stream now, she'd never find it again.

She made the laborious climb, slowly, carefully, grabbing branches, bushes, anything she could find to help keep her balance. It finally levelled off and then dropped again, down a more gentle slope. She was more clumsy than ever now. She kept pinning one shoe down with the other. Finally she stopped to rest. She thought of her friends, facing a cold night, worrying about her, and she forced herself to move even faster. It was hard to see now, and she finally took her little flashlight from her pocket, hoping there was enough strength left to the batteries for the rest of the way.

She heard the water tumbling down another steep ravine. She reached the place and flashed her light around. She sat on a rock and let tears flow freely.

"I can't face another climb. I just can't."

She dried her tears and again weighed the danger of the climb against the danger of going off into the dark woods without the stream to guide her.

She drew a deep breath, flashed her light around looking for the best route and, after deciding this slope was not as steep as the last one, started down.

Carefully she made the agonizing climb down the ravine. The cumbersome snowshoes made it so difficult to find good footholds. Her injured ankle was so weak she couldn't put her full weight on it. She couldn't use her hands to get good holds on things and use the flashlight too. She had to be satisfied with once in a while using the light when she found a solid place to stand.

It had been some time since she had used her light, and she was looking for a place to stop and rest. Her foot slipped, her hand slid off the branch she was holding, and the piece of rock her other hand held broke off. She fell, wildly grabbing the air, looking for something to break her fall. She thumped into a hard pile of snow, knocking her breath out. Yet she knew she hadn't fallen far.

She lay there catching her breath, unwilling to get up and move again. She closed her eyes with an overwhelming desire to go to sleep.

"Just a little short nap," she murmured, "then I'll move on again."

She didn't even feel the cold wind or the damp chill of the snow under her.

She thought she could hear a voice, calling, warning.

"Get up, Valerie. Get up. Move, Valerie. Get up and move."

She opened her eyes to see who was calling her. Suddenly she realized what she was doing. She got to her feet and looked around, expecting to see someone. There was no one.

"Lord, was that You?" she said. "Thank You for the warning."

She recalled being taught that there comes a point when a person will just lie down and die of exposure. She was determined to move on.

She flashed her light around and saw that she was in a sort of ditch. She flashed it toward the stream. Her heart leaped joyfully. That was a bridge! She was in the ditch next to the road. It was full of snow, but she could tell. She flashed her light up above and could see the bank where she had fallen from, the bank right over the road.

She stood on the road and tried to force her weary, dull mind to think. "I have to go in the right direction to get to the lodge. Someone might come, but I have to get to the lodge."

She made her decision and started down the road. She limped and staggered. She fell, forced herself up, and moved again. Her dull mind wondered what she would do if Jerry should come along, but she could only hope that he was hiding somewhere by now, convinced he was safe.

There was a roaring sound in her ears. She shook her head, and the sound got louder. She stumbled as a light flooded over her and the roaring stopped. She fell again as a voice said, "It's one of those kids!"

Strong arms lifted her.

She cried out, "My friends, help them, please."

"Where are they?"

"Follow the stream—there was a cabin—it burned. Please hurry—they don't have any boots."

One of the men said, "Must be the McNab mine. There's a cabin by Chambers Creek. How did they ever get there?"

"Please, help my friends."

Valerie felt herself being lifted to the snowmobile. Her hands were put around a deputy's waist.

"Hang on, young lady. We'll have you to the lodge in no time, but hang on."

She hung on and rested her head on his back, forcing herself to stay awake while they sped down Lake Road toward the lodge. They stopped and she was helped off. There was a confusion of voices; hands helped her; she was aware of warmth, then a soft bed and deep, deep sleep.

She opened her eyes. It was light in the room, not bright, but she could tell it was daylight. She tried to turn over, and pain shot through her leg. She closed her eyes again.

She tried to remember where she was. She heard a door open, and just as quickly she remembered everything. She turned toward the door in spite of the pain.

A vaguely familiar face smiled at her.

"You are awake. Good! Would you like some breakfast?"

"My friends," Valerie answered. "Have you heard—"

"They're all here at the lodge and doing fine. Cold and hungry, but that's easy to take care of. Maybe a little frostbite. They found that other young fellow, too. Dr. Triner has checked you all over. He is anxious to get you to the hospital and get that leg X-rayed, but it's snowing again, and you do need your rest. He'll have you transported later today, maybe.

"Now, the deputy has some questions to ask you, if you feel like talking. And your parents and the Peterses are anxious to see you."

"The sheriff first, I guess, to get that over with. Then my parents, please."

The lady nodded, smiled again, and left. Valerie then remembered who the lady was. She had been at the lodge when they arrived—the owner's wife.

Valerie closed her eyes. *Thank You, Lord, for Your protection and for getting us off of Slide Mountain. Thank You for Your guidance.*

She smiled as the door opened again, knowing that God would always guide and direct. And she would follow.

Frank and Joe's next case:

The Hardy brothers race to Seattle to help their father, Fenton, who stands accused of murder! In their father's rented house, they're met by burglars, who try to gun them down. When Frank and Joe follow their trail, they learn that valuable timber is being destroyed by a deadly virus. They also find that an entire town has been sealed off to prevent a mysterious epidemic.

Meanwhile Fenton Hardy is the hostage of a sinister scientist with a formula for certain death. And if the brother detectives can't reach him in time, he'll become the victim in a doomsday experiment in . . . *Disaster for Hire*, Case #23 in the Hardy Boys Casefiles™.